D0661825

.38
CALIBER

AN EMERSON DUNN MYSTERY

Roy Maynard

CROSSWAY BOOKS • WHEATON, ILLINOIS
A DIVISION OF GOOD NEWS PUBLISHERS

.38 Caliber.

Published by Crossway Books, a division of
Good News Publishers, 1300 Crescent Street, Wheaton, Illinois 60187.

Cover illustration: Keith Stubblefield

First printing, 1992

Printed in the United States of America

Library of Congress Cataloging-in-Publication Data

Maynard, Roy.
.38 Caliber : an Emerson Dunn mystery / Roy Maynard.
p. cm.
I. Title.
PS3563.A96387A615 1992 813'.54—dc20 92-6024
ISBN 0-89107-674-3

---

00 99 98 97 96 95 94 93 92
15 14 13 12 11 10 9 8 7 6 5 4 3 2 1

To my wife
and best friend Sara:
I accomplished nothing
before I met you.
Thank you.

So there I was, feeling alone in a newsroom that wasn't empty yet, looking at a blank computer screen and a dying journalism career. It was past 6 P.M. on a cold evening in January, and I was obviously past my prime. Emerson Dunn, reporter: not even thirty years old and already litter on the Highway of Life.

I reviewed my sorrowful demise. I'd awakened that morning rather uneventfully, went to work that afternoon, and saw three months of investigative reporting slip away. Before the day was out I was quoting Habakkuk and waiting for the bleak and bitter end.

Maybe I'd better start from the beginning. Three months ago I pulled cop duty two weeks in a row. It's no big deal — we just check the police blotter on Saturday to see what went on Friday night. It's usually just a couple of fights and maybe a burglary or two. Tame stuff. Not much happens in the small Texas Gulf Coast town where I live and work. Not usually. But there are exceptions. That weekend was one of them. It was a cold, mid-November weekend. Crime cools off during cold snaps, just as it heats up in the summer, so I wasn't expecting much when I leafed through the reports. But one report caught my eye.

A local gun shop had been broken into late Friday night. After neutralizing the alarm system and neatly opening locked gun safes, the burglar or burglars made off with more than fifty weapons — rifles, shotguns and pistols. Some ammunition was taken, and no prints were left.

The police immediately alerted every pawnshop in the state, but by the end of the week none of those weapons had shown up anywhere. By that next Saturday, when I pulled cop duty again, I'd almost forgotten about it.

"We had a rash of burglaries last night," Detective Sergeant Bill Singer told me as I walked into the station that morning. "Five of them. Take a look at these reports and tell me what you think."

I took the fistful of computer printouts he handed me and sat down in the detective's office. I'd known Singer since I started at the local paper, the *Times*, nearly two years before. He gave me free coffee, and I gave him free advice. Come to think of it, neither was very good.

Bill Singer was sort of a cubic zirconium diamond in the rough. His suits were polyester blends, and his ties were clip-ons, but his laugh was genuine. He was stocky, brown-haired, and a little older than me — thirty-one or thirty-two, I'd guess.

I looked down at the reports.

"Weapons," I said as I scanned them. "Lots of weapons taken. No televisions, no VCRs, no jewelry."

I looked up.

"Think they're related to last week's burglary?" I asked, knowing the answer.

"Yeah," he said. "I just don't know how. The same kinds of weapons were taken, but the M.O. wasn't really the same. Sloppy work. Window panes were broken out, gun cases opened with crowbars. No ammo was stolen, but the owners all said they didn't store ammo for each and every one of their guns, and most said what ammo they did have was kept in another room. The burglaries were not the same style as the gun shop job. But I've just got this feeling they're somehow connected."

I thought for a moment, then looked back over the reports.

"If I were you, I wouldn't worry so much about what the connection is or who's got the guns," I said as I stood to leave. "I'd worry about who they're going to. Someone is supplying an army."

"Whoa, Sherlock, don't go riding off into the sunset yet," he said, blatantly mixing his metaphors as I started to leave. What do they teach in police academies these days anyway? "What makes you think this is an arms deal?" he asked.

"No ammunition was taken in the residential burglaries, and little from the gun shop," I said. "That means whoever took the guns — whether it was one group or two — was interested in selling them, not using them. And since nothing else of value was taken, you've got to assume the burglars were simply filling an order."

If I'd been wearing a hat, I would have tipped it and left. Since I wasn't wearing a hat I just left.

Back at the empty newsroom I finished up my work and reached for the phone. It was noon, time to call in my own Dr. Watson.

"*Boker tov, Dafeed,*" I said in poor Hebrew.

David Ben Zadok, my favorite photographer and a former Israeli tank commander, groaned into the phone. "Yeah, and good Sabbath to you, Emerson," he answered groggily. "What's up? Got an assignment? You know what my mother says about me working on Saturday."

"No work — I just need some information. Get up and I'll buy you lunch."

We agreed to meet at a local coffee shop. On the way there I thought about the burglaries. There were really only two possibilities: the guns could be sold and shipped out of the nearby Port of Galveston — bound for Central America or maybe the Middle East, or they could be packed in the trunks of several cars and sold domestically.

"Great," I told myself. "It's narrowed down to two places: here and everywhere else."

I drove into the coffee shop parking lot just ahead of David and waited at the door for him. A waitress with a tattoo on one arm seated us. David and I aren't very picky as to which sorts of restaurants we frequent — although we drew the line at anything with French words in the name. None of this Cafe Le Bistro stuff. We had reputations to keep up. Wanda's Truck Stop was one of our mainstays.

"So what's up?" he asked.

I told him about the burglaries and my guesses so far.

"Take a look at my notes on some police reports Singer showed me today," I said. "Do you see anything I don't? What would these guns be used for, and where?"

He studied my scrawlings for a few moments.

"Urban warfare," he said. "Mainland America, I'd guess. Look . . . lots of .38 caliber revolvers and some bulky high-powered rifles. You don't use those in the jungle or in the desert — you use the lightweight, lighter caliber rifles. An M-16 isn't much more than a .22 caliber rifle with hotter bullets. And if these guns were for export, you'd see more 9mm and 7mm weapons. It's easier to get ammo for those overseas."

Although the weapons jargon was mostly beyond me, he'd solved the puzzle before the coffee arrived. I didn't mind picking up the tab for breakfast (or lunch, whichever it was).

Like I said, that was three months ago. How does that relate to the downfall of a potentially stunning journalistic career? Have patience — I'm just getting to the good part.

So there I was — it was late November, and I was sitting around with the knowledge that an arsenal was being readied for use. Obviously the guns were bound for some organized group — probably some gang. The only problem was that the sole gang in town was made up of some junior-high kids and a couple of dropouts. They spent most of their time striking poses outside the schools they were too cool to attend; little time was spent doing anything particularly illegal.

Still, the police department's small gang unit (small, as in two officers) was put on alert, and they were told to wear their Kevlar vests faithfully. I also prayed quite a bit. If the guns were bound for teenagers, we needed the help.

For a couple of weeks we waited. Christmas was closing in

fast, and still no sign of the guns. I began to think that maybe the weapons had been shipped out of town or out of state — until Timmy Joyce shot himself in the leg.

Timmy was an attendant at a local gas station. When the new owner bought the station from old Pete Kucek last year, he kept Timmy on even though he fired the mechanic and closed the garage. Timmy wasn't what you'd call quick. I didn't know many of the details, but some complications at birth left Timmy what they call *learning disabled* now; back then they just called him retarded. That's a harsh word, and it didn't do him justice. The schools in our small town had little to offer kids like him twenty years ago, so Timmy's mother did what she could — which ended up being much more than the doctors ever expected. Timmy could do quite a bit for himself. He even landed a job at Kucek's gas station.

He must have been some sort of a tax write-off or at least a good PR move for the new owner — or maybe he was just cheap drudge labor. But Timmy didn't seem to mind.

He swept up, emptied trash cans, and ran errands for the — ahem — *interesting* sorts of attendants the new owner hired to run the place. The town's last full-service station became just another corner convenience store, selling only premium and unleaded gasolines and overpriced groceries. Of course, when the new owner wasn't around, Timmy would still check your oil for you.

When I heard he'd shot himself, I went straight to the local hospital. I found Timmy and his mother Anna in the emergency ward. Timmy was sitting on one of those beds with paper sheets, flashing a wide grin to the nurses as a doctor covered his stitches with a Snoopy bandage. I smiled too. Timmy was younger than me by only two or three years, but sometimes I think he got the better deal. Timmy had the mind and the faith of a child — and few of the worries of an adult.

"Timmy, what are you doing playing with guns?" I asked. "You know better than that."

His smiled faded.

"I know, Emerson," he said. "But I just wanted to look at it. It wasn't like Mr. Pete's gun."

Obviously, I thought to myself; this one was loaded. Pete Kucek always kept a pre-World War II pistol around, but I don't think it ever left the drawer under the cash box. And I know for a fact it was never loaded. Pete's wife hid the bullets long ago, probably before Timmy and I were even born.

It wasn't until I left the hospital and actually drove past the gas station that it hit me: the new owner had installed a silent alarm and a bulletproof window. Why would he need a gun there? And why in the world would he leave it with Timmy — or with any of the other semi-transients he'd hired to man the cash register? I figured I'd better stop in for some gas and maybe a little reconnaissance.

I pulled up to the pumps, once again amazed that no one carries regular leaded gasoline anymore. Of course, the execs at Exxon would probably have been just as amazed that any cars needing regular — such as my beat-up '74 Ford — were actually still on the road. But I valued my car, an old Galaxy. It had the all-important trailer hitch and an eight-cylinder engine, and it was heavy — perfect for pulling a sailboat from my apartment's carport to the ramps at Galveston or Clear Lake. During the nine months per year you could sail in this area, that was great. I was reminded, as I stepped out of my car and noticed no change in apparent temperature, that the lack of a working heater made my car a bit less perfect during the other three months.

This place had only two pumps, and the only one working pumped premium-grade gas. I checked my wallet to see if I was ready for such an investment, then went inside to pay before pumping.

"Evening," I said to the clerk. "Give me five dollars of premium."

The clerk grunted. He was a big, muscular youth, just out of high school, I guessed. A second glance made me amend that thought; his nearly shaved head made him seem younger at first, but on closer study he seemed to be in his mid-twenties. He was watching a sitcom on a small black-and-white television set perched on the counter. He wore the typical gas-station-attendant work shirt, which announced to the world that his name was Frank. Frank was doing his best to ignore me.

"Catching 'The Cosby Show'?" I asked.

He sneered. He either disliked Cosby or disliked me, and I got the feeling it might have been All Of The Above. I smiled again and went to pump my gas. The owner obviously hadn't gotten a gun to protect *this* guy; this overage skinhead looked as if he could take care of himself.

The next morning I called Bill Singer. I found out that Timmy hadn't been able to adequately explain where he'd found the gun; he just said it came from the garage. The bullet that was taken from Timmy's thigh proved to be a small-caliber slug — a .32, according to Bill.

"I called the new owner — he said he left his pistol in there by mistake," Bill said. "His story stank, but not enough to justify a search warrant. I'm at a dead end."

"Let me see what I can do," I said. "Maybe I can get in — legally, of course."

Bill grunted, then told me to watch myself. I hung up and dialed David's number.

"I need some more help, buddy," I said when he answered. "Can you be here in half an hour? And bring a yarmulke."

When he showed up twenty minutes later, he wasn't wearing the Jewish head covering I'd asked him to bring. When I asked him about it, he pulled a bright blue one out of his jacket pocket.

"Yeah, yeah, I've got it," he said. "What for? You think you need to go to synagogue and pray? You're a Christian! You want to be a Jew?"

I laughed.

"Look, Dave, I'm not even very good at being a Christian," I said. "I doubt I'd be much better at being a Jew. Besides, the yarmulke isn't for me, it's for you. Now let's go make some trouble."

We drove to the gas station. When we arrived I told David to put on his yarmulke and try to look harmless.

"Slouch a little, zip your jacket up all the way," I said. "You know, look like you get beaten up by your sister on a regular basis."

He frowned at me.

"What are you up to?" he asked with some justification.

"Trust me," I said with no justification at all.

We walked into the station. The television set was still on, but last night's skinhead had been replaced by another one. This guy had the same shaved head and stocky build, but added a menacing look of incomprehension to the ensemble. His shirt told us his name was Benny.

"Excuse me, but I think I got some bad gas here last night," I said. "Sounds like water in the tank."

"Sounded fine when you drove up," he said with a glare. His eyes were a little crossed, so I couldn't really tell if he was glaring at me or at David.

"Well, it's not," I insisted. "Why don't you be a good boy and pull it into the garage over there and drain the tank. It won't take you ten minutes."

"Sorry, pal, but our garage is all locked up. No can do. But why don't you go on home and have your Jew-boy here do it for you?" the punk said with a smile.

I heard David's breathing quicken, so I nudged him, hoping he'd get the message and behave — for now.

"Is your boss here?" I asked. "I can see that he's not. Why don't we give him a call and let him know about our little problem, hmmmm?"

The skinhead sneered in response.

I smiled sweetly. "Or else I'll let my friend here correct your vocabulary. This 'Jew-boy' doesn't take too kindly to that kind of language. And you'd better watch him — the last fight he was in was called *Beirut*."

David — also smiling, but not as sweetly — stood up fully and leaned his six-feet, two-inch frame over the counter.

The clerk glared and grumbled, but reached for the phone. He covered his mouth and the phone with a hand so we couldn't make out many words, but the way he spit out the word "Jew" was unmistakable. He finished the conversation and hung up.

"Mr. Sandersen wants you to leave," he said. "He said for you to take your car to a garage somewhere else and have the work done. Then send him the bill. He don't want no problems."

"That could get awful expensive. I know some very costly mechanics. Is he sure he doesn't want you to do it? We could even push the car into the garage and take care of it ourselves, couldn't we?"

"He don't want no one in the garage," the punk said. Then he paused. We didn't budge.

"If you don't want problems, you'll do what Mr. Sandersen says. Me and my friends don't like this kind of behavior from Jews and Jew-lovers. I think you need to learn your place, and I got lots of friends to help me teach you."

I had to pull David by the arm, but I succeeded in getting him out the door without any gratuitous violence. Although I'm sure he would have appreciated doing just a little violence to the skinhead.

"Look, David, we got all we needed," I said as we drove off.

"What? Humiliated?"

"No . . . information. We know that this new owner, Sandersen, has something in his garage he doesn't want the public to see. And we know there are a few neo-Nazis running around without their hair. What's that add up to?"

David thought about it for a moment.

"The weapons?"

"Right," I said. "And if I'd have let you take that jerk apart, his buddies would be burning more than a cross on your lawn."

David mumbled a few Hebrew curses and said something in English about being able to handle a few brainless bigots. I didn't doubt him at all.

But even if the weapons were in the garage, we didn't have enough for Bill to get a warrant. A surly skinhead does not a D.A. impress. But I was sure — and the thought of a well-armed skinhead gang was terrifying.

The one thing I didn't know was who had stolen the guns in the first place. These new-wave Nazis weren't bright enough to crack a safe or neutralize an alarm system. I bet they had trouble running a gas station. I was stuck, just as Bill had said.

But that night the burglars hit again.

"They cleaned out two private gun collections," Bill said the next morning. "They hit the first house between 3 A.M. and 4 A.M., then the second between 4 A.M. and 5 A.M., we think. Some neighbors were nosy enough to notice activity going on around that time, but they didn't bother to call us. Again, no ammunition. And this time they got some automatics."

"Just what we need," I said. "What's the total now?"

"More than a hundred weapons in all," Bill told me. Then as a perverse afterthought, my favorite cop added, "Have a nice day."

I walked out of Bill's office, through the squad room, and into a deep case of confusion and despair. I drove the four blocks from the police station to the newspaper office with the radio off and my thoughts on hold.

But as I pulled into the paper's parking lot, it hit me. If the last break-in occurred at 5 A.M. or so, it was probably too late to make a delivery to the garage. Too many people would be out and about driving to work — especially since the chemical plant (the town's largest employer) began its first shift at 6 A.M. The gas station sat right on Highway 6, which leads west to the plant. Surely they wouldn't risk being seen unloading an arsenal at that hour. Thus there was a good chance the drop would be made tonight.

I had a city council meeting to cover, but I knew David was free. All I had to do was talk him into watching a gas station full of racists all night — and convince him to refrain from filling them with premium unleaded.

"But, David, we're talking Pulitzer stuff here," I begged about an hour later at Wanda's, our favorite coffee shop/truck stop. "You use that ASA 3200 film, get some covert shots of them unloading weapons, we print it in the morning edition, give the negatives to the D.A., and we're heroes."

I knew I had him. I handed him a roll of 3200 — night film, the kind we used at poorly lighted high school stadiums during football games. This film could pick up whatever was going on without the use of a flash. David smiled.

David has the journalist's *drive*. You can teach someone to write a news story in the classic inverted-pyramid style, but you can't teach him (or her) to be a reporter. That's something that comes from inside. It's a need for truth, a drive to help make things right by bringing them out into the light. David had it. I had it. At times we both wished that we could get rid of it. Maybe someday they'll make an antibiotic for it.

"OK, I'll stick around there for a few hours," he agreed. "Maybe we'll get some pictures, maybe not. You owe me one."

"I owe you several, to be exact," I said.

The city council meeting was the usual drab stuff. The council approved a new storm drainage system for one of the older subdivisions in town, and some lady complained that her trash wasn't being picked up regularly. The meeting let out about 10 P.M., about the same time the second shift ended at the chemical plant. I went back to the office, banged out about twelve inches worth of council news, checked the pages, and gave Jimmy the OK to take this edition to the printer (few of us smaller papers have our own presses — we used the one at our sister paper a few towns over). As usual, Jimmy complained about the time (I was fifteen minutes past deadline, but he'd have complained if I'd been on time anyway). He left, and I was alone in the office.

I ran a fresh pot of coffee through our eternally soiled machine and filled an equally unsanitary thermos. David had said he'd park around the back of a closed-down restaurant that sat across from the gas station on the small state highway. I drove over, and as I neared the restaurant and gas station I turned out my headlights (no one else was on the highway). I didn't want to be seen frequenting an eatery that had been closed since before I'd come to town. That just might cause some valid suspicion. I drove my Ford into the parking lot and around to the back of the restaurant, where I found David's battered Toyota.

David wasn't in it.

"Dave? Buddy? Pal? Please come out from wherever you're hiding and tell me you didn't do something stupid like go over to try to get a closer shot. This is why God gave us telephoto lenses for our cameras, Dave. David?"

Nothing. I felt a blackness in my stomach as I inched over to the side of the building to get a better look at the gas station.

I saw a white van and a car, but neither was parked at the pumps. Lights were off in the station, though some light came from the crack at the bottom of the closed doors of the two-bay garage. The garage and station were separated, but the two buildings were only a few yards apart.

On top of the gas station lurked a figure that could only be David Ben Zadok, looking down at activity going on behind the garage.

David probably felt perfectly safe, snapping away frame after frame atop the gas station. And maybe he was. So I sat back against the side of the restaurant, watched, and waited. The night was getting colder by the minute. I decided to pass the time by cultivating an ulcer.

Soon I saw three men coming out of the darkened gas station. They got into the van and drove off to the west, away from town. The car remained.

"What's up?" I suddenly heard David's voice from behind me. I hadn't even seen him climb off the building and cross the highway.

"Nothing's up. I'm just sitting here watching my best friend do something really really stupid, that's all," I snapped. "What was that? Getting on top of the building? And exactly where were you going to run to if they saw you?"

"They didn't see me," he said. "Don't worry. And who said anything about running?"

He grinned that grin again, and I knew for a fact that this guy is the photographer I want to have with me if I ever cover a war. That is, if he isn't the one who started it.

"So what did you get?" I asked.

"Boxes," he said. "The van came, the men in it met some blond guy in a suit, they unloaded cardboard boxes into the garage."

"Just boxes?" I asked. Cardboard boxes wouldn't convince a D.A. of anything, and they aren't very photogenic either.

"Maybe. I got one shot of something else," he said. "I'm not sure. I had to hold my camera below the awning, point, and guess on the focus. Let's go back to the office and get these rolls developed."

I nodded, looking back out at the gas station across the street. The car hadn't moved. We got into our own cars and drove slowly around the restaurant, with our headlights off. David, in front, pulled onto the highway and headed back east toward town and the newspaper office. I did the same. But as I pulled the switch to turn on my headlights, a car behind me did the same.

It was past midnight now, and there had been no cars on the highway. This one had obviously been watching us and waiting.

"*Oy vey*," I said to no one in particular.

There's a verse in the Bible about walking through the valley of death and fearing no evil. It was King David who wrote it, as a matter of fact. The thought occurred to me that this was the same David who, armed with a slingshot, took on a giant. Trouble was, I was no David.

The headlights behind me flashed. I sped up, closing in on David's Toyota. I hoped he'd get the message and gas it. He apparently did, after a moment of bumper-to-bumper tension. He sped up, and I sped up. I looked down at my speedometer; it read 75 mph. Unfortunately, the car behind me was still closing in, coming within a few car lengths.

Then my rearview mirror exploded with blue and red flashes.

I let out the breath I didn't know I'd been holding. A cop. That was the first time I'd ever been grateful to be nailed violating traffic laws. I slowed down, pulled over to the side of the highway, and watched David's taillights disappear into the night. In my side mirror I watched the cop walk towards me.

Emerson? I think you'd better follow me to the station," came a voice I knew. It was Tom Brewer, an investigator. "Detective Sergeant Singer would like to speak to you."

"Fine, detective," I said. "Lead the way."

Apparently David and I weren't the only ones watching the gas station. Chances are, Brewer had spotted us as we left the restaurant and called in. Bill would have known it was us — but he wasn't going to be happy about our little outing.

We took the Commerce Street exit and drove south to the downtown area. When the police car drove into the "Department Personnel Only" lot, I veered off into the "Visitors" lot. I walked in through the front door of the admittedly shabby cinder-block building and on into the waiting area. A dispatcher sat behind a bulletproof window and a wall of electronics. She recognized me and spoke into an intercom microphone, then motioned for me to sit down. I felt like I was waiting for the school principal to emerge.

Then he did.

I'll spare you the stream of adjectives, modifiers and gerunds that Detective Sergeant Bill Singer lavished upon me. Translated into proper English, his words would have been something to the effect of, "I must say, I'm disappointed that you and your charming friend would endanger an ongoing investigation. The possible ramifications of said entanglement include obstruction of the justice that both you and I crave, as well as possible jail time for you and your friend. By the way, did you get any pictures?"

That last part was pretty much verbatim; whenever he asked me for photographic evidence Bill was notably less profane. I was feeling cooperative. Or at least I thought I saw a way out of the boatload of trouble I seemed to have found myself in.

"Let's go see," I said. "I bet David's got the negatives drying by now."

Bill grunted, made a gratuitous comment about the likely professions of several of my ancestors, and agreed.

"We'll take my car," he said. "I want you back here with me when we're done."

Maybe my escape plan wasn't fool-proof, I realized. But some good shots might get Bill in a better mood.

We drove to the newspaper office and found David's car parked there. We let ourselves into the building, and I went back to the darkroom and knocked on the closed door.

"Dave? It's me. I've got the cops here. I sure hope those pictures are good."

"I'll have contact sheets in five minutes," he said through the door.

I went back out to find Bill looking through my desk.

"Looking for contraband?" I asked.

"Actually I'm looking for some aspirin," he said. "You owe me. You're the cause of this headache."

"Top drawer, next to the antacid," I said.

I keep a generous supply of both. Journalism is a stressful profession, OK?

A few minutes later David emerged with a handful of contact sheets, showing a positive image of each negative from what must have been five rolls of film.

"Nothing but the car and van, license plates and boxes," David said with some disappointment. "Except for this."

He laid one sheet on the desk and pointed to a frame that

clearly showed two men studying an object, an object that less clearly seemed to be a weapon.

"Uzi," David said.

The outline was faint, and the object seemed to just be a dark splotch to me.

"Can you blow this up?" I asked.

"I did. Here." He produced one more 8-by-10" sheet with an enlargement of the negative. It was an Uzi, all right. I'd seen enough Secret Service men and their weapons of choice during my career to know that this wasn't the smaller pocket version of the Israeli automatic either.

"That's the real thing," said Bill. "That's a heck of a weapon."

David snorted. "In Israel that's a girl's gun," he said. "In the army we used Galils. More firepower."

"Yeah, and you used a tank too," I said. "That still doesn't change the fact that we've got clear evidence that automatic weapons — at least this one — are being unloaded into a gas station. That's got to be illegal, right? Bill, what's next?"

Bill studied the photo.

"They do make a semiautomatic version of the Uzi that's perfectly legal," he said, still looking at the photo on the desk. "Still, I think we have enough for a search warrant. I need two copies of each of these photos by morning."

Before David or I could protest, he looked up.

"There are, of course, less pleasant places for you two to spend your night than in the darkroom," he said. "You get these prints to me first thing in the morning, and I'll forget that you two interfered in a police investigation and broke several state and federal laws. Good evening, gentlemen."

That Detective Sergeant Bill Singer. What a guy.

With bleary eyes and hands smelling like darkroom chemicals, David and I drove to the police station just after 8 A.M. I'd left a note on my editor's desk that I was calling in dead for that day. I planned to sleep soundly. David dropped me off at my car, still resting safely in the department's parking lot. Then he went into the station to drop off the photos.

I got into my car and turned on the radio as I pulled out. The all-news radio station was talking about the fresh gang war that had erupted in Houston; Hispanic gang members were blowing away Asian gang members and vice versa. Five drive-by shootings in the past three days. I reached down and turned off the radio. I wasn't in the mood.

I drove the rest of the way to my small apartment in silence. The radio and police scanners were the last things I wanted to hear. My apartment, the upstairs floor of a 1929 two-story home, was about five blocks from the police station (the other direction from the office). I lived in what was once the nice part of town; in fact, in 1929 this was the nicest house around. But neighborhood decay had set in after the 1950s, and the Ewens, the elderly couple who had built the home for themselves, now rented it out as two apartments. The house didn't have many years left; it had survived two floods and three hurricanes, but time was about to bring it down. I wasn't sure it would pass inspection if the city ever took the time or effort to inspect anything in that part of town.

But such a deal on the rent!

I climbed up the steep set of stairs that was tacked onto the side of the home when old man Ewen divided the house into two apartments. The stairs had a faded warning at the bottom of them stating in effect that the owner of the house and the builder of the stairway took no responsibility for anyone's safety. Luckily there were enough double negatives in the hand-lettered warning to make that statement pretty questionable in court if push came to fall.

My downstairs neighbor, a fast-food restaurant manager, was just leaving for work as I unlocked my door. I waved and wondered for the jillionth time how he managed to smell like french fries *before* he went in to work. None of my business though.

I went inside, tossing my jacket on the first available piece of furniture, which happened to be the kitchen table. It was, like I said, a small apartment. I hit the flashing button on my answering machine to listen to my messages.

"Emerson, this is Remington," came a threatening — but nice — female voice. "Call me. You have both numbers. We need to talk about this gun burglary thing. I think you're holding out on me, you jerk."

You wouldn't expect to hear such a nice voice from a girl who called herself by her last name. I knew her for six months before I discovered what her first name even was. A reporter for the other newspaper in town, the *Courier*, she used her initials in her byline: A. C. Remington, staff writer.

She told me once that she just thought it shouldn't be an issue to her readers whether she was male or female, so she preferred using initials. I could see that. I also suspected it had something to do with the fact that her first name was Aggie. College loyalties are a force to be reckoned with in Texas; her father had attended Texas A&M and was obviously proud of that fact. Go, Aggies!

Out of sheer spite, it seems, Remington the Younger attended A&M's arch-rival school, the University of Texas.

Remington was a nice-looking girl. She was about 5'6" and a couple of years younger than me. She had dark hair and blue eyes. She didn't use her looks to get ahead though. I never once caught her batting her eyelashes at a cop to get just a little more information, or smiling sweetly at the mayor to warm him up on a touchy issue.

She was at a little bit of a disadvantage in that her newspaper came out only once a week while mine came out twice a week. She had to do in one Thursday paper what our paper and somewhat larger staff did in a Thursday and a Sunday paper. It couldn't have been easy, but she still gave me some tough competition.

I wasn't up to arguing with Remington that morning. If she was mad now, she'd be furious if she knew we'd given photos to the cops. That would probably make the photos public information and she'd demand copies. I thought it best to ignore the message and go to sleep. I walked through the kitchen into the living room and made it as far as the couch. The bedroom door was open, and I saw two weeks' worth of laundry piled on the bed. *Maybe I'd better just stretch out on the couch for a while,* I thought.

I awoke to the sound of a fist banging on my door.

"Emerson? Open up!"

"Only if it's the police," I groaned. "And only if you promise to shoot me."

"It's not the police . . . it's worse! I don't care how sick you are . . . you're holding out and I know it! I've seen the pictures!"

The sweet, almost soothing voice of A. C. Remington drifted through the cracks around the front door like a stiff winter wind. I looked up at my clock; it was nearly 10:30 A.M. I'd only been asleep for two hours.

I got up and unlocked the door. Outside stood Remington, with a grocery sack in one hand.

"Come on in," I said. "My home is your home."

"I knew it," she said, brushing by me into the kitchen. "You're not dead. You're not even sick. Sharon told me you probably wouldn't live to see noon. She said you were deathly ill."

Sharon, our receptionist, was willing to cover for me, but she wasn't very good at it. We went to the same church, so I guess I couldn't fault her for being good at being honest. I ought to try it myself sometime.

Remington dropped the grocery bag on the kitchen counter. I went over and looked in. Impressive. Cans of soup, crackers, a bottle of orange juice, and flu medicine.

"Forget it," she said. "I'm taking it all home with me. You're not sick — not physically at least."

"OK . . . so what brings you to my humble abode?" I asked.

"You know why I'm here. Singer showed me the photos. He's typing up a report right now, and as soon as he gets it over to the judge's office he'll have a search warrant. Now, what do you know that I don't know?"

I pulled a chair out from my slightly precarious kitchen table and sat down. Remington didn't need an invitation to do the same.

"Nothing, really," I said. "I think the gun burglaries are related, but there's no evidence that they are. The first was a very professional, very slick operation. A safe was cracked, not blown open. The alarm system was neutralized, not smashed. The burglaries after that were all of the smash-and-grab variety. Lots of things broken, very messy operations."

"So what makes you think they're related?"

"The same kinds of weapons were taken, and nothing besides the weapons were taken. They didn't care about the ammo, and they didn't care about the TVs and VCRs they passed on the way to the gun cabinets. It just seems like they're filling an order."

"So where does the gas station fit in?"

"I think they're stashing the guns there," I said. "So after the burglary a couple of nights ago we watched the place. They made a drop, David got some pictures, and it seems I was right."

"You *hope* you're right," she said. "Singer is running the warrant this afternoon. He said he'd let us come. If this pans out, it could be one heck of a bust. If it doesn't, Singer isn't going to be too happy with you."

"I could have figured that part out on my own," I said.

I made some coffee as we chitchatted about the city council and other less interesting subjects. I would have liked to get some more sleep before we went with Bill to search the garage, but Remington seemed glued to that chair. She didn't trust me, I guessed, and didn't want to let me out of her sight between now and then.

Or maybe she liked my coffee and my sense of humor. Yeah, right.

The phone rang at about 11 A.M. I picked it up before the answering machine kicked in. It was Bill.

"Dunn, we got the warrant," he said. "Find your buddy Remington and let her know we move at 2 P.M. If you guys just happen to be around the gas station about then, you might see something worth writing about."

"Right," I said. "Let's hope so."

I put down the phone and looked at my watch. Three hours.

"That was Bill," I said. "He's serving the warrant at 2 P.M. He told us to be there. So what now . . . are you buying lunch?"

Almost three hours later I was following Remington's Volvo down State Highway 6 (really just a glorified four-lane divided thoroughfare) toward the gas station — and what was going to turn out to be a very bad afternoon.

She slowed, entered the turn-lane, and pulled into the gas station. I started to do the same, and as I did so I caught in my rearview mirror a glimpse of a familiar Ford LTD Crown Victoria police special. Bill's car was an unmarked black model, but it still screamed "I'm a cop car!" to the world.

I turned into the gas station and parked off to the side of the building. Remington had pulled up in front of a pump and was trying to look as if she really intended to buy some gas. A moment later my favorite detective sergeant pulled into the lot, followed by two squad cars. I saw the attendant grab the telephone.

"Dunn, imagine meeting you here," he said. "And your pal Remington. Did you know her first name was Aggie? We had to call the Department of Public Safety's driver's license bureau to find that out. I lost a $10 bet on it. Anyway, let's go serve a warrant, shall we?"

Bill got into these sorts of things — warrants and searches, arrests and what-not. He obviously enjoyed being a cop.

He marched to the front door of the station and smiled at the attendant. It was Benny, the second skinhead I had met. I didn't know if he recognized me.

"I'm Detective Sergeant Bill Singer, and we have a warrant to search these premises. Please unlock the garage."

"Wait until my boss gets here," the skinhead said dully. "He's on his way."

"Doesn't work that way," Bill said. "Now open the garage. Officer, help him."

Escorted by a patrolman, the punk walked through the small storeroom and out the back door of the station, then over to the back door of the garage. He pulled some keys from his jacket pocket and unlocked the door.

"Go ahead," he said. "But my boss will be here any minute, and he ain't going to be happy."

Bill motioned to one of the patrolmen to watch the attendant while he and the three others entered the garage. Remington and I walked past the skinhead, who sneered at us.

"I don't see badges on you two," he said.

"It's OK, Benny," I replied. "We're with the band."

We followed the cops into the garage. It was a box of a building, really. Just a tall cinder-block construction long enough for two bays and deep enough for a Chrysler or even a '74 Ford Galaxy and a mechanic or two. Sometime after it was built, hydraulic lifts had been added; now the lift platforms sat on the floor and would probably never again expose the underside of a car. The gray walls were empty; not even a single tool-company freebie calendar graced them. The garage's two bay doors looked old and feeble; quite a bit of rust was visible on both.

While the patrolmen searched the almost-empty shelves, under the bare tool benches, and behind the dozen or so old metal barrels, Bill went straight to the six or eight oblong cardboard boxes stacked on top of one of the old lifts. I looked over at Remington, who was beginning to frown.

Bill took out a pocketknife and slit open the top of one of the boxes. He peered down for a moment, then reached in. He didn't seem pleased with what he found.

Yard signs. He pulled out a handful of political yard signs, all made of bright plastic. They were already stapled to wooden stakes, ready to be pounded into lawns across the city, declaring to all that Mike Sandersen was running for city council.

I started feeling a bit ill.

The next box held yard signs too. These said in bright red and black letters, "Crime: Sandersen can stop it."

We were raiding the political stores of a man running on a law-and-order ticket!

"Can I help you officers? I'm Michael Sandersen. I'm the owner." The voice came from behind me. I jumped. I get a little nervous around suspected arms dealers but downright jumpy around would-be politicians. Sandersen was a tall, blond man, probably about forty-five or so. He wore a suit, he was clean-shaven, he had a good smile and a firm voice. He'd sell to the voters.

"I'm Detective Sergeant Bill Singer," Bill said with a touch of embarrassment in his voice. "We have a warrant to search this property. We also have some photos we'd like you to explain."

Remington and I tried to blend into the woodwork. But I'd already become part of the investigation, so when Bill quickly wrapped up the search and followed Sandersen back into the gas station, I followed too.

Once inside the gas station, Sandersen walked behind the counter and turned to face us.

"Now what's this all about?" he asked.

"We obtained these photos of boxes being unloaded at about midnight last night," Bill said, pulling the pictures from a coat pocket. "A strange time for the delivery of campaign materials."

Benny mumbled something about all this being Timmy's fault; Timmy had drawn attention to the place. Benny and his coworkers probably blamed a lot of things on Timmy. Sandersen motioned for Benny to be quiet and turned back to Bill with a smile . . . a snake's smile.

"The printing company is owned by a friend, and he and his boys did these for me after he closed up shop yesterday," Sandersen said. "They brought them over just as soon as they were finished — I was anxious to see the signs."

"And what about this?" Bill said as he produced the photo of two men — one of whom was obviously Sandersen — examining the Uzi.

"Payment," Sandersen said, again with a smile. "Rich gave me a good deal on the signs, I gave him a good deal on a gun. I'm a part-owner of the gun shop too, you know."

The stunned silence told me that Bill *hadn't* known. But then I hadn't either, and I'm supposed to be a good investigative reporter.

"Is there anything else, officer? If not, I'd like to get back to work. We're gearing up for Christmas. Should be a good year for gun sales this year, with the crime wave we're having and all. As a matter of fact, it was the burglary of my gun shop that prompted me to run for city council. Maybe you should be out trying to find the person who did it and leave the law-abiding public alone."

I looked over at the skinhead, who stood grinning next to his boss.

Bill grunted something about "We're following some leads on that" and left with his entourage. Remington and I followed the cops out the door.

"You're in trouble so deep you'll never surface, Dunn," Bill said lightly as I passed him on the way to my car. "I want you in my office within the hour."

I nodded. I looked over at Remington, who wore a slight grin.

"He'll get over it," she said. "But until he does, I'll come visit you in jail every day."

I shrugged — the only response I could think of — and walked to my car. On the way back to the office I thought about where I'd gone wrong. Maybe I'd made too great an assumption when Timmy found that gun and shot himself. If the owner of a gun shop has a weapon or two lying around the gas station he also owns, what's the big deal? Obviously I should have done my homework.

I parked at the newspaper office and went in. Sharon started to say something, but saw the look on my face and thought better of it. Everyone was in the office — the ad sales reps, the accountant, my editor, the other reporter, the sports guy, and the publisher. David wasn't around, but that wasn't unusual. David was the most dependable photographer around, but not always the most visible. He was usually out on assignment, and when he had no assignment he was out cruising for feature art — you know, photos of families buying Christmas trees with the littlest kid pointing up to the biggest tree in the lot, that sort of thing. He did most of his darkroom work in the late, late evenings since the chemicals in the poorly-ventilated darkroom had a tendency to stink up the entire building. So when we wanted David during the day, we usually beeped him. It worked out OK.

"How's it going, Emerson?" asked Barney, my editor. Barney was a nice guy, though none too ambitious and never one to let hard work get in the way of lunch or any other activity that interested him. He was easygoing, but that seemed to sit well with the publisher, who wanted a newspaper that refrained from making too many waves. It got a little frustrating for me sometimes, but I couldn't help liking Barney.

Steve, the other reporter, just nodded at me as I slumped into my chair, across from his desk.

"It's going fine," I answered. "Except I'm probably going to jail for a few years. Can you hold my job open for me?"

"Not a chance. What was it . . . drugs . . . gambling? . . . Or did they nail you for that last column, complaining about the coffee at the police station?"

"Photos," I said. Steve's eyebrows shot up, and Barney grinned.

"It's not like that," I said. "David and I got some shots of some guys unloading boxes at the gas station out on Highway 6. We thought it might be linked to the gun burglaries. Singer caught us watching the place, demanded copies of the photos, and on the basis of those got a search warrant. It didn't pan out."

"We know," came the voice of Mr. Andrews, the publisher. I hadn't seen him come out of his office — in fact, I hardly ever saw him come out of his office. This wasn't a good sign.

"I just got a call from Mike Sandersen, who's in my Rotary Club," Andrews said. "He says he's having a press conference at 4 P.M., announcing his candidacy. He told me about your little raid."

He turned to my editor.

"Barney, have Steve cover the press conference," he said. "Emerson's had a busy day. And, Emerson, I want an update on how construction's going on South Commerce Street. Twelve inches by morning."

Rule One with publishers is, don't embarrass them in front of their Rotary Club buddies. Barney had given me a warning when he hired me. "Check your facts very carefully," he said. "If you make a mistake in a story, Andrews's cronies will give him a hard time at Rotary Club the next week. Three Rotary ribbings and you're toast." And there wasn't much we could get away with; the mayor was in the same Rotary Club, and so was Captain Edward Clark, the police department's second-in-command. If I made a mistake in a council story, the mayor knew it. If I made a mistake in a cop story, Clark knew it. So I always checked my facts very carefully. Except this time.

Mr. Andrews, a gray-haired man of about sixty-seven or sixty-eight, walked back into his office to await the next crisis. That's what publishers are for, I guess. Barney looked almost sympathetic. "He's the boss," he said profoundly.

Steve looked miserable. Steve had been on staff for a grand total of three weeks now and was fresh out of college. He was just getting comfortable with writing about the school board and covering their relatively tame political machinations. I was sure he didn't like the idea of covering something like this, especially when it was my beat.

"Buck up, Stevie," I said. "It'll be easy. I'll be here pretty late tonight, so I'll give you a hand if you need it."

Barney turned back to his computer terminal, and Steve just nodded at me. I grabbed a notebook and left the office, bound for the South Commerce Street project office (a trailer at the job site) and for the police station, to answer to Detective Sergeant Bill Singer.

I figured I'd better go by and get the information I needed from the South Commerce Street project engineer before I went to see Bill. There was no telling how long he'd want to gripe at me. The construction project update was really a garbage assignment — that's why I got it. I knew I'd have to take two paragraphs' worth of information — "we're still on schedule" — and turn it into twelve inches of copy. I got into my car and drove out of the parking lot, pulling onto Cedar Street, which crosses Commerce. I took a left and headed south on Commerce to where the street narrowed for the widening project.

Fifteen minutes later I was driving back north on Commerce, having learned that "the project is still on schedule." It was time to meet my fate. I drove up to Oak Street, turned left to head west toward the police station. I looked at my watch. It was a little past the hour Bill had given me to show up in his office. But maybe he'd be in a better mood and would have started to see the humor in the situation.

Boy, was I wrong. Then again, it wasn't as bad as it could have been. He didn't shoot me.

Again I'll spare you the details of his diatribe. Let's just say he thought it best that I stick to reporting the news, reading the blotters, and keeping out of police business. He did admit he'd made some mistakes — like trusting me. After a thirty-minute interview he let me leave. Remington was just coming into the station to read the day's reports. We passed each other in the hallway.

"Keep away from Singer," I said. "He's had better days."

"You look like you have too," she said. "You'll be in your office later?"

"Much later. Sandersen is a Rotary Club buddy of Mr. Andrews, so Mr. Andrews isn't happy with me, so I'll be putting in some extra hours to make up for it."

She nodded and went on her way. I rubbed my eyes. I'd been steaming ahead since yesterday with only two hours' worth of sleep, and tonight promised to be a long one. On the way out I also passed by the open door of Captain Edward Clark's office.

"Dunn," he said, "come in here for a moment."

Since cops, even captains, are generally armed, I complied. I didn't want to. The captain was not one of my favorite members of the force. He had that ambitious look in his eyes, the kind that makes you wonder just how far someone will go to get what they want.

I sat down in a rather plush leather chair. The chair and mahogany desk said a lot about Clark, I thought. So did the immaculate hair (thinning and graying a bit, but always neat and perfectly trimmed). So did the wool suits. Clark dressed for success, and he decorated for success. You don't put a mahogany and leather desk-and-chairs set in a captain's office unless you're planning to move them into the chief's office in the near future. I wondered if the chief had noticed that.

"You were wrong about Mike Sandersen," Clark said. "Now, you and I have a good working relationship, and I'd like to see you develop the same with Mike. He's a good man if you get to know him. A good man. Let's all three have lunch sometime. I think you'll see what I mean."

"I guess I was a little off-base," I said. "Yeah, I'd like to meet him under better circumstances. Give me a call whenever you want to do it."

"I will," he said rising. He shook my hand in the way a politician would. "That's all I wanted to say."

He sat again at his desk and forgot I was there. I left the office and walked out of the station.

I checked my watch. It was nearing 5 P.M. *I might as well swing by my apartment and grab some dinner before going back into the office for the evening,* I thought.

A few minutes later I was hitting the sofa in a full-body slouch (a tricky gymnastic maneuver, I might add) and listening to the soothing hum of a microwave oven. I closed my eyes and let my thoughts drift . . .

Remington . . . A. C. Remington . . . I wonder if she's ever fired a gun . . . I wonder what the C stands for, considering the A stands for Aggie . . . I wonder if she's ever driven a car that takes regular leaded gasoline . . . I wonder if Sandersen has ever fired a gun . . . Probably . . . He could be a champion marksman for all I know . . . But his part-ownership of the gun shop is obviously an investment . . . If Bill hadn't known about Sandersen's involvement, that means Bill only talked to the majority-owner of the shop when the burglary occurred . . . The silent partner had remained silent . . . Bill hadn't done his homework either, it seems . . . "Crime: Sandersen can stop it" . . . Quite a campaign promise from someone who owns a gun shop and a gas station . . . But if he's never at the gun shop and he's never at the gas station, what does this guy actually do?

My eyes snapped open, and my attention snapped to attention. I reached for the phone and dialed hurriedly.

"Levine Investments," a woman answered.

"Andy please," I said. Soon Andy Donaldson's tired voice slurred a greeting. Andy, an investment broker, did the bulk of his work early in the morning when the stock market was open. By 5 or 5:30 P.M., he was usually pretty beat.

"Andy, I need some information on an investor, one of those guys that doesn't do anything else," I said. "His name is Sandersen . . . Michael Sandersen."

"What do you need this for?" Andy asked.

"The guy's running for city council, so I thought we'd better check him out," I said. "Besides, your father-in-law will be calling you soon for the same information." The last statement was pure conjecture on my part . . . journalistic license, so to speak.

"Wrong," Andy said. "I just got off the phone with Sam. If I don't have the lowdown on this guy by tomorrow, I'm out of the family."

Andy had the dubious honor of being married to the mayor's daughter. Mayor Sam Barton, a politician of the old school, was obviously grooming Andy for city office — the planning commission first, then a council seat. That's how I met Andy. Sam dragged him to every council meeting, so I usually sat on the back row with Andy and Remington, shooting the breeze while the council argued insignificant points of whatever zoning case was before them. Sometimes, just to let the council know we didn't take them too seriously, we'd order pizza. The mayor always glared at us when the Domino's delivery man arrived.

"I'll call in twenty-four hours," I said. "The next pizza's on me."

I went into the kitchen to see about the neglected burrito still lying in the microwave. I didn't mind eating alone, and I didn't really mind living alone . . . although I guess I was starting to feel a little envious of Steve. Steve lived with his parents. He made great grades in high school, went off to college and earned a journalism degree, then came back to work on the hometown newspaper. His parents were thrilled. He said he felt like he was coming back to be sixteen again. Only now he went off to work instead of to class.

He seemed a little lost, even though he'd grown up in this town. I felt almost guilty about it, but I saw Steve as sort of a misplaced child at a shopping mall. Things I didn't think twice about mystified him. For example, the first time I took him to the police station with me he was visibly (and understandably) bothered by the foul language used by some of my closer police friends, but he was also bothered by their guns. I could tell by the way he kept staring at them. Some of the younger cops were guys

Steve had known in high school. Not that he had spent much time with the kind of kids that later become cops, but he at least knew them by face and name. But their guns seemed to scare him . . . Or fascinate him.

Steve not only seemed a little lost, he also seemed a little lonely. While he came back home after college, most of his friends went on to bigger and better towns. Houston, thirty-five miles away, drew most of Steve's friends into its grimy downtown heart. The math club crowd and the debate team buddies Steve had hung around with in high school were now fresh accountants or law students. He was a reporter at the hometown newspaper, but he wasn't satisfied. He seemed to want more. Much more.

Still, his mother was there to iron his shirts and feed him meals from a real oven, not a microwave, and he was able to save money by living at home. I made the right sympathetic noises when he'd complain about being treated like a kid again, but I really didn't feel that sorry for him. He talked about getting an apartment, but his parents always convinced him to stay at home a little longer, to save just a little more money. I thought they were right.

It wasn't only that Steve looked younger than he actually was — he was also a little green. Naiveté doesn't last long in this profession; you learn very quickly that people aren't a particularly nice bunch. Unless as a reporter you're just a "cheerleader," you're going to run into a sensitive issue at some point, and that wonderful politician of whom you think so highly is going to turn out to be a schmuck. Even the best are only human. Steve hadn't been disappointed enough yet to realize the truth in what preachers have been saying since Moses' day: everyone has a little bit of bad in them. Maybe that's why so many of us journalists are confirmed cynics. I didn't really think Steve was ready to be alone in the wild world; not yet anyway.

My own parents lived in Dallas, about six hours away by car.

I didn't see them nearly as often as I would have liked to. But I guess it gets that way when you get older.

Now David . . . this guy had it made. He lived with his mother and stepfather. His mother, also an Israeli, had been widowed in the Six Day War in 1967, when David was three years old. She'd stayed single for years, until a charming American petroleum engineer working in Israel swept her off her feet.

"It was just like a movie," she told me once in her wonderful thick accent. "He came and took me away to America. My uncles, they made him buy me a round-trip ticket just in case. But I will not need the return ticket."

David was already in the army when his mother left, and he stayed in Israel long enough to get a degree from Tel Aviv University. And then, as soon as he could, he joined his mother here. He told me he was tired — tired of the constant threat of war, the constant threat of terrorism. He said he was tired of the compulsory service in the reserves (three months out of each year), and he was tired of trying to make it in an economy that saw double-digit inflation yearly. Here he found a sanctuary. He found a job, he worked hard, he ate his mother's cooking, and he even found a girlfriend — during one of the weekly trips he and his mother made to the kosher markets in Houston.

Ruth was working behind the counter of her father's deli when David met her. She'd just graduated from college with a degree in business and had big plans to run a vast deli empire she'd build with her dad. She was slow to realize that her plans weren't going to work out. You could see it in the way Shlomo did business — the way he greeted each customer by name, the way he gave "special deals" to the widows and treats to the children. The only empire he wanted was his one small deli over which he could reign.

Ruth didn't know what she wanted — but she knew when she saw this dashing young Israeli war veteran and photographer that he'd seen enough of the world to show her some of it. David saw a pretty American girl who listened to his stories and didn't make him wear suits too often.

Their dates usually either began or ended at my place, with the three of us discussing great and glorious things. The thirty-minute drive to Houston to drop her off — even late at night — was worth it, David said. He liked this girl.

My burrito suddenly tasted a little cold and dry. I dumped it in the trash can, grabbed a jacket, and headed for the office.

About an hour later I was wrapping up my construction story when Steve came in.

"I'm really sorry, Emerson," he said.

"What for?"

"For taking your story," he said. "I didn't want it."

"Don't worry about it," I told him. "I made Mr. Andrews mad, and that's his way of showing it. You were just in the wrong place at the wrong time. Do you have the story done?"

"Yeah . . . It's in the system," Steve said. "This Mike Sandersen seems like a nice guy."

"Oh, he's a peach, I'm sure," I said.

I called up the story on my computer screen. Barney had already coded it and put a headline on it. It was a banner — it would go on top of the front page. Nothing but the best for Andrews's cronies. I read through the story and found that Sandersen did indeed sound like a peach of a guy.

Running on an anti-crime platform, he was sure to get the endorsement of the powerful Police Officers Association. Steve called him a "local businessman," although he had some investments in Houston and other towns as well. He'd never been involved in politics, at the local or any other level, but "this wave of crime made me mad enough to want to do something." Sandersen was married but had no kids.

"The article looks great," I told Steve. "But remember, we only give them the first one. The rest they work for. The first article that comes out, announcing their candidacy, is bright and shiny and above all positive. After that, we make them sweat. Got it?"

"What do you mean, sweat? Work for what?"

"Well, look at this paragraph," I said, pointing to the screen. "He says he'll give the cops the resources they need to fight crime effectively, and he says he'll hold the line on taxes. Next time you ask him how, if he plans to hold the line on taxes, he plans to pay for the new police equipment. He'll answer that he'll cut the fat out of the city budget. Then you ask him what fat he means and where exactly he would cut. I seriously doubt he has an answer for that, and that's exactly what we're here for — to give him heck."

"He sounds like he's thought all this out," Steve said. "He sounds like a good guy."

"He'd better do more than just sound good if he's going to be setting the tax rate for me and you and your parents and everyone else in this town," I said.

A knock came at the front door to the office. I looked up at the clock; it was about 7 P.M. Steve unlocked the door and let in our favorite competitor.

"Just checking on you," Remington said as she came in, visibly straining to see what article was up on my computer screen.

Steve looked nervous — The Enemy Amongst Us and all that. "You think it's OK for her to be in the office like this?"

"Lighten up, Steve," I said. "It's after-hours. Besides, she couldn't keep up with pros like us even if we gave her copies of our articles a week in advance."

"Yeah, well, you boys ate my dust on the civil service petition last week, didn't you?" she said. "And I believe your Thursday paper was amazingly free of any mention of the hold-up at Whataburger."

Steve started to protest but stopped when I laughed.

"Come on, you two, let's go get some food," I said. "And, Steve, your loyalty should always be to the profession, not to any particular paper. A newspaper is a business and must be run as a business. A journalist's function is more than to just make money for that business. Be loyal to the facts, not to the morning edition of the *News*."

I switched off my terminal, grabbed my jacket, and followed Steve and Remington out the door. Steve was still frowning.

"Uh, I think I'd better go on home," Steve said. "I already ate . . . with my parents. You two go on."

As Steve got into his Pontiac (a four-door, a definite dad's hand-me-down car), Remington nudged me.

"Good speech," she said. "You believe that garbage? You know I'd rip your throat out and walk on your grave for a chance to scoop you guys."

It's your gentle way with words that charms me," I told her. "Are you up for some dinner? I'm starved, and it's been a really bad day."

"Sure. I'll buy."

I began to adjust to this assertiveness of hers really quickly — especially if she was buying me food. I like that in a person. We drove to the only real restaurant in town (at least the only one where you didn't have to clean your own table when you were done). It was run by two brothers named Walter and Gunther Schmidt. They were Germans who served mostly Mexican food. Go figure. But for me they'd whip up a *jaegerschnitzel* and some kraut. They always had fresh coffee ready, and they had that European habit of coming and sitting with customers for a chat.

Sometimes late at night, when I'd gotten the paper out and they were cleaning up for the next morning, I'd go and bang on their door. They'd let me in, and we'd grab a booth and some coffee and unwind. They explained to me that they'd come to town by way of Mexico, where they had run a restaurant also. A prominent Hispanic attorney in Houston was a regular customer of theirs (when she was down in Mexico visiting relatives), and when she handled the foreclosure on this restaurant she decided to buy it and let Walter and Gunther run it.

It had to be losing money. I mean, it was never really crowded.

But maybe that was changing; it had a slowly growing clientele. I, for one, was slowly growing myself. If it hadn't been for these two guys I'd have died long ago of Excessive Microwave Burrito Consumption.

"*Guten abend,*" I called out as we entered the empty restaurant. It was about an hour before they officially closed, but they were already cleaning up. No customers were there to distract them. "Coffee, and make it quick. We don't have all day."

"Ja, ja, we hear this all the time from you Americans," Walter said as he escorted us to a booth. "Hurry up, I have a meeting — hurry up, I must go soon — hurry hurry hurry. Why do I work so hard to make good food? You Americans eat it too fast to tell. I could give you frozen dinners and you wouldn't know. Your tongue wouldn't be able to protest before you were thanking me for the quick service."

This was Walter's biggest gripe with the country, and it was also his usual topic of conversation. He had another sore spot too.

"And I'd like some ketchup for this here German-fried whatchamacallit . . . ah, weenersnitzel," I said. "These things always need ketchup."

He moaned, wrung his hands, and started sobbing something in German — a lament about my pagan ways, no doubt. Gunther appeared from the kitchen with four cups of coffee, telling Walter in poor English to stop whining and see to the potatoes.

"You do this on purpose, I know," Gunther said as he set all four cups on the booth's table. "Why do you do this? You wait, he comes now with a speech on how he makes food to be savored."

I grinned. Remington was looking at the four cups of coffee for two customers. Apparently she hadn't been here before; she didn't know it was customary for them to sit with us. Walter, potatoes presumably seen to, came out and joined us at the booth.

"The food I prepare, it is to be savored, tasted," he said. "I am a chef, I have been to school, I am not a machine to make fast food."

"You're in the land of automatic teller machines and drive-through everything," I said. "But, Walter, I enjoy your food — I savor it. Have you ever seen me rush through one of your meals?"

Remington spoke up.

"Can we please see a menu?" she asked.

I laughed.

"They're almost closed," I told her. "Menus are only for when they're open. Now they fix whatever we want. The only catch is, we have to help them wash up afterwards. Remington, this is Walter and Gunther Schmidt. Boys, say hello. Remington works for the *other* newspaper."

"It is very nice to meet you," Gunther said. Gunther was at first the shy one — he was less sure of his English than Walter. But lately Gunther had been speaking up a little more, especially when young women were around.

"I've driven by here dozens of times, but I've never stopped in," she said. "You have the inside fixed up so nice. I remember when this place was a catfish restaurant — it was a real dump then."

"You're telling us from dump? We spent one month cleaning before we could move our ovens in," Walter said. "In Germany, if a man had a restaurant like that he would go to jail."

I had to admit the restaurant was fastidiously clean. Let me put it this way: Dylan Parks, the city's health inspector, came here for lunch nearly every day. Need I say more?

"So what may we prepare for you, Emerson?" Gunther asked.

"Bring us your specialty, with everything," I said. I looked at Remington, who nodded in a sort of confused, distrusting way. Why don't people trust me?

Gunther's specialty was *jaegerschnitzel*, "hunter's steak." It's basically a pork chop with vegetables and mushroom gravy poured on it. But the mechanics of the words do no justice to the reality; it was wonderful, sort of a symphony in your mouth. And it was especially good here. No German restaurant I'd ever found could compare to what these boys could do in a Mexican restaurant.

Gunther went into the kitchen to start our dinner, while Walter, Remington and I talked for a while. Then Gunther called to Walter and mentioned burning potatoes. Walter sighed. He shook his head and left for the kitchen. Soon we heard rising German voices and the clattering of pots. Remington looked nervous.

"Great guys, as long as they're not in the kitchen at the same time," I said. "Then they get in each other's way. It's OK as long as we hear pots banging around, but let me know if you think you hear cutlery."

Emerson, I'm sorry about this afternoon," Remington said, looking into her cup of coffee. "You thought you had him, didn't you?"

"I thought so. I was wrong."

"I covered the press conference. I'm not so sure you were wrong."

"What do you mean?" I asked.

"He's a snake. I don't know why I feel that way, but he gives me the creeps. His wife never said a word. She just got out of the car, stood at his side, and smiled. He said all the right things, and he seems to have the right background, but something just doesn't fit."

"I don't know. I'd like to meet him, talk to him. I'd like to see if he can look me in the eye."

Gunther came out with two plates heaped with schnitzel, potatoes and — unannounced but never unwelcome — Walter's apfel strudel. Walter brought us glasses of water and silverware too. Such service.

"Now we will leave you alone," Walter said. "We must finish up in back."

He nudged Gunther, who reluctantly complied.

"Nice guys," Remington said. "I wonder why I haven't tried this place before."

"Maybe because the outside of it still looks like a gas station-turned-catfish restaurant," I said. "There's not much they can do about that; it *was* a gas station. But they've done what they can with the inside. And I bet they'll go all-out decorating for Christmas — German-style. It'll be something to see. It was really something last year."

"Where will you be for Christmas?" she asked. "Are you sticking around here or going home — wherever that is?"

"Home is in Dallas, I guess," I said. "At least that's where my parents are. I'll make it up there for a couple of days, but we still have to put out a paper the next Sunday. How about you?"

"I don't know. I hate holidays. They always make me choose."

"Choose?"

"Who to go see," she said. "For the first few years after my parents' divorce, it was easy. The judge said who I'd spend each holiday with. I was with Mom on Thanksgiving and Dad on Christmas one year, the opposite way the next year. But now I'm all grown up, and I have to decide those things for myself. Not much of a choice, though. It's either go see my mother, which I'll probably do, and listen to her talk about well how her codependency class is going and how she's forgotten all about Dad; or go see Dad and his new family — the trophy wife and the stepbrother of death. Dad's new wife wears too much makeup, and she has this son who's obsessed with death. He wears only black and listens to music about suicide, and he really seems to like funerals. I avoid the whole scene there as much as possible."

"Where do your mother and father live?"

"They're both in Houston. Mom's on the north side. She got stuck with the house they bought twenty years ago when the neighborhood was nice. She can't sell it for a decent price now. Dad's in a really nice condo near Rice University in the fashionable part of town. Real mid-life crisis stuff, right?"

I nodded. There didn't seem to be much to say, so I listened some more. I usually find that if you let them, people will talk to you. Remington seemed willing to do most of the talking that night.

"It really doesn't bother me, though," she said. "Mom got the house, a car, child support for my sister and me until we were eighteen, and Dad paid all of our college bills. At first I thought Mom had really raked him over. But that was more than ten years ago, and it's so much different now. He's successful, he's got a new family, and he seems happy. She's still changing the color of her hair every week and answering phones for an insurance company."

"She has her two daughters," I said.

"No, she's got me. Not Sandra. Sandra was always a daddy's girl. She cried in the courtroom when Mom got custody of us. She spent as much time with Dad as she could. She's in New York now, but when she comes home for the holidays Mom will be lucky to see her for fifteen minutes. But I've stuck by Mom."

I looked down at Remington's plate. She'd only moved her dinner around a little on the plate with her fork, sort of like an unambitious hockey player. She hadn't eaten a bite. I called for Walter.

"*Ja, ja, Herr Dunn, was ist los*?" he said, playing the part of the dutiful waiter.

"Micro-nuke her plate for a few seconds to warm it up, please," I said.

The German bowed and took her plate. Remington looked a little embarrassed.

"Really, it looks wonderful," she told him. "I was just talking too much."

He took it back to the kitchen and reemerged in a few moments. The plate was steaming again, but it wasn't the same plate of food. I should have known. A man like Walter would never serve reheated food — he would prepare a new plate. Remington realized this too and looked even more embarrassed.

"Your dinner again, miss," Walter said curtly. "But this is fresh; we do not reheat."

That was too much. It was time to step in.

"You old *hausfrau,*" I said. "I bet if we looked in your dumpster we'd find hundreds of foil trays. You buy this stuff from the freezer section at Kroger, don't you?"

That set him off again. A full five minutes later, after a lecture about the pains he took over the hot stove and the nights he stays up until all hours scrubbing pots and preparing kraut, he stormed back into the kitchen. When he didn't immediately emerge holding anything sharp, I knew we were safe.

"How'd you get to be such a special customer?" Remington asked.

"Goose," I replied. "Specifically, Christmas goose. Last year these poor immigrant boys were stranded in southeast Texas with no family and not many friends. I came in one afternoon, and I asked them what they missed most. They said goose. They told me they'd looked in every grocery store in town and couldn't find a goose to roast. They said they missed their families, but they could call on Christmas day. And they missed the snow, but not *that* much. What they really missed was the smell of cooking goose. They said it just wasn't Christmas without that. Well, I knew David was taking his mother into Houston the next day to stock up on kosher food for Hanukkah, so I tagged along. At this European market I found two of the most beautiful, fat geese you'd ever want to roast. I brought them back, marched into the restaurant, and told the boys that if they cooked one for me they could have the other one. You'd have thought I'd given them plane tickets to Deutschland, the way they went on. So I drove up to Dallas with this steaming roast goose — garnished with apple and filled with this beef-based stuffing — on my front seat. My dad was just as goofy about it; he'd been in Germany in the army in the 1950s and had goose for Christmas then."

"What a sweet thing to do," she said.

"No . . . I had completely selfish reasons. You should have tasted that goose."

A few hours later, after Remington and I helped wash our dinner dishes and she and I went our separate ways, I found myself staring up at the unmoving ceiling fan above my bed. I was bone-tired, but for some reason I couldn't sleep. Something was troubling me — or maybe I was just sensing the trouble that lay ahead.

I don't know when I dropped off to sleep. I do know that it was noon when I awoke. That wasn't a huge problem. Thursdays are light days for us since we really didn't put the Sunday paper together until Friday. Usually I spent Thursday dropping in on my sources — checking police reports and the latest political gossip. It wasn't unusual for me to not make an appearance in the office until after lunch on Thursdays — the time I put in late Friday nights made up for it. The company was getting its forty hours out of me, and usually more.

I called Sharon to check on the Status of Things. Sharon, our forty-five-year-old receptionist, was good about always knowing the Status of Things. She could tell by the way Mr. Andrews made his coffee what kind of mood he was in — she said she could tell by the volume. Not the amount of coffee he made, mind you, but the amount of racket he made while making said coffee. If he banged the pot and cups around, she knew he was in a rather bad mood. Such things may be rather obvious for some, but not for me.

"Good morning, Sleeping Beauty," Sharon said as I greeted her. "I hear you had a date with the competition. Up late? You know, A. C. just broke off her engagement a few months ago. She's probably about ready to start looking again."

Sometimes Sharon knew more than was good for her . . . or for me. I hadn't even known Remington had been engaged. We had sat through council meetings together every week for almost a year, and she never mentioned an engagement. And she certainly never mentioned that she'd toasted the guy, whoever he was.

"It wasn't a date . . . we just got some dinner," I said. "I didn't know she was engaged. How do you know these things?"

"It's a small town," she said. "Besides, my sister's husband is the accountant for that paper. I have my sources too."

"You should have been a reporter. Anyway, how are things up there? Has anyone noticed that I'm not in?"

"No one. Mr. Andrews has a doctor's appointment in Houston, so he's out all day. And Barney left for lunch at 11 this morning and told us not to expect him back. The only one of you guys that's still hanging around is Steve."

"It must have been Steve that told you about last night, the rat."

"Wrong. I had an early lunch with your German friends. They wanted to know who the beautiful young woman you were with was."

"They only said that because they've been here over a year now and neither one has had a date."

"So you'd better make your move soon, Emerson. You might have some European competition. Walter's a little too old, but Gunther's about your age, isn't he?"

"Gimme a break," I said. "I don't need this. I don't have any moves to make. I don't need a girlfriend . . . I need a bottom-floor apartment so I can bring my dog down here from my folks' place."

"Speaking of which, you got some messages," Sharon said.

"My dog called? I knew he'd figure it out as soon as my parents got rid of that rotary-dial phone. How's he doing?"

"No, not your dog, your mother," she said. "She wants to know if you've written your grandmother, if you've sent your niece a birthday present, and when you're coming for Christmas."

"Why didn't she call me at home?"

"I told her about your late night with a beautiful girl. She said it was about time. She said she'd let you sleep. Call her when you get a chance. And she mentioned a food processor, if you haven't thought of anything to get her for Christmas yet. I told her you hadn't. Really, we had a nice talk."

"That's good to know, Sharon. Any other messages?"

"Yes, call your buddy Bill Singer. And that's it."

"Don't expect to see too much of me today," I said. "If Paula gripes, tell her it's only Thursday and I have thirty-six hours in already."

Our associate publisher Paula doubled as our personnel supervisor and our accountant. They gave her the nice title in lieu of a nice salary. She wasn't very happy with that, and she wasn't very happy with our department (i.e., the editorial department: me, Barney, Steve, and Will, the sports guy). The only thing that made her more angry than a reporter's weird hours was paying overtime for those hours. She was convinced that our jobs could — and should — be done in a forty-hour, 8-to-5 week, like jobs in the real world. There was simply no way; this was news, not the real world.

Wait. That didn't come out right. But you know what I mean.

I hung up the phone and debated calling Bill. He probably just wanted to yell at me some more. I'd call Mom tonight when rates were cheaper, but I didn't have the same excuse for Bill. So I dialed his office's direct number.

"Yeah," he answered.

"I got your message," I said. "What's up?"
"Emerson, Timmy Joyce was killed last night."

In half an hour I was showered, dressed, and down at the station. I walked into Bill's office. Without a word he handed me a report. He looked like he'd been up most of the night; he probably had.

It seemed that a simple armed robbery had gone bad. According to the attendant, Timmy had been watching the gas station while the attendant went to do some work in the garage. It was about 10:30 P.M., he said, when he noticed a car pull up in front of the station. The attendant didn't think anything of it and figured Timmy could take care of the customer. But a few moments later, the attendant said, he heard a single gunshot. He rushed out of the garage in time to see a car pulling out and speeding away. Timmy was on the floor, bleeding from a wound in his chest. He was dead by the time the ambulance arrived.

The cash register had been opened and emptied. They got away with probably around $150, the report said. The cops couldn't put down an exact figure since the attendant said he had no idea how much money was in the register. The register was old, he said, and wasn't the kind that kept track of its own income. What a way to run a business.

I sat down.

"This is full of holes, Bill," I said. "Everything about this guy's story reeks. This attendant — this Frank Johnson — he's one of the skinheads, right?"

"Yeah."

"What work was he doing in the garage? You saw it; it's empty. No tools, no cars, the lifts don't work anymore."

"He said he was sweeping," Bill said.

"Right. This punk is going to sweep a filthy garage and leave Timmy to mind the store. Bill, Timmy's the only one who has cleaned anything in that place for the past five years. They've kept him on specifically for that purpose — so they don't have to get their hands dirty."

"I know, Emerson, but . . ."

"Get this punk in here! If he ran out of the garage right after he heard the shot, he'd have been able to get at least a description of the car. What's this garbage about the car going too fast to get a plate number? The idiot probably just doesn't know his ABC's or his numbers."

Bill stood up.

"Dunn, calm down and sit down. We're working the case."

I sat. Bill was right; ranting wasn't helping.

"OK, what was he shot with?"

"Looks like a .38 caliber or a .357 Magnum," he said. "We're not sure yet. We'll have the medical examiner get all that for us. Emerson, we know how to do our jobs."

I nodded and stood to leave. As I walked through the door and started to shut it behind me, Bill stopped me.

"Timmy's mother is pretty shaken up," he said. "She's a member of your church, right? We had an officer drop her off at home last night after she identified the body, but as far as I know she didn't call anyone. You might want to give the pastor a call and make sure he knows. Do what you can, Emerson."

I nodded and left.

The office was fairly quiet when I arrived. Steve was staring at a computer screen, Sharon was taking a classified over the phone, and Paula, Barney and Mr. Andrews were nowhere to be seen. Donna, an ad salesperson, was on her way out the door when I walked in.

"We've gone up four pages on the Christmas edition," she said as I passed.

More good news. Four extra pages of white space to fill, just so they could get more ads in. Well, I told myself, it could be worse. Having too many ads is definitely the better problem to have. It just meant more work for the editorial department.

Sharon started humming "White Christmas" — in reference to the white space Barney always complained about and I always filled — when she saw the look on my face.

"What's wrong?"

"Timmy Joyce was killed last night," I said. "The gas station was held up. He was shot in the chest."

Sharon nodded. She reached for the phone — to call Timmy's mother, I'd bet. Sharon and Anna Joyce weren't that close, but they'd taught Sunday school in the same church for years. I made it to my desk and reached for my own phone.

"Martin please," I said when the church secretary answered. "This is Emerson."

Martin Paige was the pastor of the small Bible church I irregularly graced with my presence. He was more than that to me; he'd been there at the right time when I started to realize that my life was missing something — life, to be specific. I had been a twenty-two-year-old who felt like a zombie, just going through the motions of living until my body realized what my soul already knew: I was dead. Martin helped show me there's more. That was five years ago. For the first two of those years he pastored a small church outside Dallas and helped me along. Within a year I was teaching Sunday school myself and considering a career in the ministry. For a while there I thought I had all the answers. Now I knew I didn't.

A year ago, just before my own engagement was broken, I got the job down here, and the distance brought out what I told myself would have been a fatal flaw in my marriage to Julie —

namely, that the relationship was based on the fact we kept each other entertained, and little else. Martin found himself and his family down here as well. Maybe God was trying to look out for me; or maybe He was just mad at Martin and was making him put up with me a while longer.

"Emerson? Long time no see," he said. "Susie's been asking about you."

I smiled. Susie was the world's cutest baby, Martin's youngest daughter. I'd been with Martin the night she was born. He was speaking at a revival in Fort Worth, and I had gone with him. We made the long drive back to Dallas in much less than record-breaking time after he got the call that his wife was in labor. He wouldn't let me speed. Being a pastor, I guess he was funny about laws and stuff like that. It got on my nerves sometimes. And as for Susie . . . I had this feeling that she'd always have me wrapped around her little finger. It was so much nicer to think about Susie than the reason I called. But back to business.

"Martin, Timmy was killed last night," I said. "Armed robbery at the gas station. Sharon is checking on Timmy's mother."

There was silence at the other end of the line.

"Emerson, I need you on this one," Martin said after a pause. "Just like the old days. Anna doesn't have any other family around here, so I'll need you to take care of the funeral arrangements. I'll take care of Anna."

"You've got it," I said. "I'll drop by your office later."

We hung up, and I looked down at my unkempt desk. Under a file on the city's thoroughfare plan I found my phone list. I flipped through it until I came to Wally Moore's number.

"Wally, this is Emerson," I said when he answered from Moore Funeral Home. Wally had been an unsuccessful candidate for city council last spring, and I had suspicions he was going to make another bid this year. He ran the family business, but he wasn't the somber, eerie sort you always imagine would run a funeral home. He was actually pretty personable — and a good candidate. He hadn't lost by much, and I'd told him I thought he could win if he tried again. Again, back to business.

"Wally, Timmy Joyce was killed last night. The medical examiner's going to autopsy the body, but I need you to take care of it after that. Do you know where Timmy's father is buried?"

"He's in the old Republic Cemetery," Wally said after a pause. "I'm looking at a chart now."

"Can you put Timmy near him?" The Republic Cemetery, with graves dating back to 1836 (when Texas really *was* a republic) and earlier, was reserved for the older families in town. Most had family plots which had been purchased long ago, so space was probably pretty tight.

"I think so," Wally said. "Yeah, Tom Joyce bought two spaces — for himself and Anna, I presume — but there's one on the other side of him we could use."

"Perfect," I said. "Let's set the funeral for Saturday. There's not much family that has to come in from out of town, so that should be enough time. How's 4 P.M. look for you?"

"Open," he said.

"Go with your standard casket, but do what you can to economize. We don't know what Anna's financial situation is. This one might be on the church. Check Tom's marker and get something to match it. That'll be on me."

"No, that will be on the house, Emerson," he said.

"Thanks. If you have any questions, give me a call. If there are any changes, I'll call you."

"Emerson, will I need pictures?"

Knowing what he meant, I cringed. "No, Wally, I don't think so. It was a chest wound, so his face should be fine. When you pick the body up from the county, check it though. Give me a call."

As I hung up the phone I wondered if Martin and I weren't being a little pushy in taking care of someone else's family business. Still, the last thing Anna Joyce needed was to hear a mortician asking if he'd need pictures to reconstruct her son's face.

"Saturday at 4 P.M." was a pretty standard time; I knew that's when Martin liked to schedule funerals. If Anna Joyce wanted something different, of course we'd change it. But most of the time, Martin always told me, people appreciated someone taking care of all that for them. It's part of the church-family concept Martin was so sold on.

It took me quite a bit of time to write the story about the robbery and murder. When I was done I checked with Sharon. She had stayed on the phone with Anna until Martin arrived. Bill was right — Anna hadn't called anyone. She'd just sat up all night in her lonely living room staring at a family photo from years gone by when there *was* a family.

Sharon then mobilized the most effective force in any church: the Little Old Ladies. I knew that by tonight Anna would have a refrigerator full of casseroles and a house full of company. Martin always said that visitors were good; grief needs a friend or two around, he said. He was right. Grief by itself becomes destructive.

"I'm sorry to hear about what happened," Steve said.

I turned. I'd forgotten he was there; or more exactly, I hadn't really even noticed him.

"Yeah . . . Timmy was a good guy," I said.

"Wasn't he the retarded guy who worked at the gas station?"

I paused. I didn't like to think of Timmy that way, but I guess he was.

"Yeah."

"That's sad — to think they killed him for less than $150. I hope you put that in your story. Probably some black kids out of Houston," Steve said. His sympathy was a little unconvincing. He turned back to his work.

I grabbed my jacket and started out the door.

"Will you be back today?" Sharon asked.

"Doubt it. I'll be in early tomorrow though."

Christmas was two weeks off, but the outside temperature was still about 55 degrees. Walter and Gunther laughed at us thin-blooded Texans for wearing coats on days like this. But this afternoon more than the temperature made the day seem bleak and cold.

I navigated Commerce Street again to the south part of town, passing Remington's office. Her Volvo was in the parking lot. A Volvo on a journalist's salary could mean only one thing, I suddenly realized as I passed: her sister wasn't the only daddy's girl in that family. A Volvo is the kind of car a daddy gets for his daughter because they're extremely safe — you have to make an effort to get hurt in a Volvo, no matter what kind of wreck you're in. Sure, they're expensive, but Daddy's Little Princess is worth it, isn't she? Remington wasn't as tough as she made out.

When I reached Border Street — which, as you might guess, was once the south border of town — I hooked a right and headed toward the church. Valley Bible Church. There wasn't a valley anywhere in sight, but let's not get technical.

Martin's car was in front. The Little Old Lady Brigade must

have relieved him at Anna's. I looked at my watch. It was nearly 5 P.M. I wondered where the afternoon had gone.

I walked through the front doors of the small church. To the right was the hallway leading around back to the Sunday school rooms, and to the left were the offices. Straight ahead was the sanctuary. I turned left and found Martin sitting on a desk talking with one of the deacons — Gene Harris, owner of a local plumbing company.

"Emerson, it's good to see you," Martin said with a sincerity that made me feel a little awkward.

"Saturday at 4 P.M., right?" I said. "That should give family time to get here."

"That's fine," Martin replied. "But there won't be any family. Anna's only sister is too sick to come. It'll just be us."

I nodded. "Does she — does she need anything?" I asked, not wanting to use the word *money*.

Gene stood.

"We think so, Emerson," he said. "I did some plumbing work for her last month; the check bounced. She was all aflutter about it and wanted to bring me cash right then, but I told her to keep it. Just some clogged pipes . . . nothing major. But I think that was a sign she's having some money problems."

"I told Wally to send the bill to the church," I said. "I've got a little money set aside if that's a problem."

Martin shook his head. "That's what the benevolence fund is for," he said. "Don't worry about it. You've been a great help so far. But there is another need . . . Can you take Anna's class for a few weeks?"

Thunk.

This was it. For everything bad I'd ever done, this was the burden dropped upon my shoulders from above. I felt a cold numbness in my brain as two terrifying words came to mind: junior high.

Anna taught the junior high class and now . . .

"Martin, I haven't been to church in weeks," I said.

"Months," he replied.

"Exactly. Are you sure you want *me*?"

"Positive. Find a helper, though. That was always Timmy's job. He was big enough to sit on any kid that got out of line."

I had this sudden vision of David Ben Zadok in a Christian church using Israeli commando moves on a rowdy junior high class. Effective, I thought. But his mother would have a fit. I was about the only *goy* — Gentile — she thought much of.

"I'll find someone to help," I said. "Yeah, I'll do it. You plan these things just to get me back into the fold, don't you?"

Martin smiled that pastor's smile, the kind that makes you wonder what he knows that you don't.

"Not me, Emerson, not me."

Friday was uneventful. I called Andy at about 3 P.M. and found out very little about Sandersen. Apparently Sandersen had a deal with the big bankruptcy attorneys in the region. If the right kind of business went under and went to one of these bankruptcy firms, they'd call Sandersen. Sandersen would offer to step in and bail the business out. He'd pay the lawyers a finder's fee — equal to or more than what they'd have earned from filing the bankruptcy — and go in as a silent partner. He liked gun shops; he owned parts of seven of them in the area. He also liked jewelry stores; he had an interest in three of them.

But that was it. Andy had little background on him. I thanked him and hung up.

We got the paper out by midnight, and Barney and Steve left as soon as the pages were out the door. Will, the sportswriter, had finished early and was long gone. David and I hung around, talking.

"So what do you think about Timmy's murder?" David asked. "I know he meant a lot to you. Think they'll catch whoever did it?"

"A cop once told me that a murder case gets cold faster than the body does," I said. "If they don't have some definite leads within twenty-four hours, chances are the case won't be solved.

In this case they don't have a description of the person or persons, and they don't have a description of the car. It's just another armed robbery."

I didn't feel like talking about it much. The funeral was the next day, and I was a pallbearer. I wasn't looking forward to it.

I told David I had to get some sleep, but he said he wanted to stick around the office to get a head start on next week. I drove home through the cold night, thinking about the Christmas decorations on businesses and homes along the way. Some were gaudy, but I didn't mind. I wondered if Christmas decorations offended David. I'd have to ask him about that sometime. He'd probably laugh and tell me he didn't mind a bit that we got so worked up about the birth of a fine Jewish rabbi.

At home I checked my answering machine. No messages. *Good*, I thought as I hit the couch. *And the crowd goes wild. The judges rate that magnificent full-body slouch a 9.5, sports fans. Clearly Olympic material . . .*

My "alarm" Saturday morning was the telephone ringing less than two feet away from my ear. I tried to open my eyes but was only slightly successful. Not only had I gone to sleep on the couch again, I'd left my contacts in. My eyes hurt, and my whole body ached. I answered the phone.

"Emerson, it doesn't add up," Remington said. "I think I can find out more."

I groaned into the mouthpiece.

"I think this Frank Johnson guy is holding out. I know you think I always think someone is holding out. Well, it's not paranoia. I know men. If he knows anything more, he'll tell me. He goes on duty at noon. I'm going to stop in and see if he'll talk to me."

I groaned again. She wasn't getting the message.

"Did I wake you up?" she asked.

"Yeah. What are you going to do?"

"I'll just ask him a few questions."

"What makes you think he'll talk?"

"Men like to brag," she said. "You can eat my dust on this one."

"Yeah, well, be careful," I said, slowly waking up. "Remember, one of those skinheads knows you're a reporter. The guy Benny, the one that was there when we ran the warrant with Bill, will recognize you."

"Don't worry about me, Dunn. I can take care of myself."

She hung up. I looked at my watch, which was by now permanently embedded into the skin on my wrist. It was nearing 10 A.M. The funeral was at 4 P.M. I had a little time.

Breakfast consisted of a bagel and some juice. I read the Houston paper, took a shower, and started to watch an old movie on my black-and-white television set. Before long it was time to head for the church.

I don't remember much about the funeral. I guess I was too busy checking details to become emotionally involved. Martin read a passage from the Psalms; not the 23rd that everyone knows, but a different one — Psalm 40. I'd read through it before, I'm sure, but I'd never paused and taken it in.

> I waited patiently for the Lord; and he inclined unto me, and heard my cry. He brought me up also out of a horrible pit, out of the miry clay, and set my feet upon a rock, and established my goings. And he hath put a new song in my mouth, even praise unto our God; many shall see it, and fear, and shall trust in the Lord.

Timmy trusted. Martin trusted. But could I trust that Timmy's murderer would be caught and convicted? His death seemed unrelated to the gun burglaries; those paled in comparison. I hadn't thought seriously about them since Thursday morning when I heard the news about Timmy. But I couldn't help feeling there was some kind of link.

I drove one of Wally's white Cadillacs from the church to the cemetery. It was packed with teary-eyed friends. I tried to ignore them. Ironically we drove right past the gas station on our way out Highway 6. I didn't want to look, but from the corner of my eye I saw a blue Volvo.

Remington was there.

She's a big girl, I told myself. *She knows what she's doing.* I drove on.

The graveside service was brief. I couldn't avoid Anna any longer, so I went up to her as she stood with Sharon and some of the other ladies from the church. Anna was a stocky, gray-haired widow who'd been given more than her share of sorrow. Timmy's early years were hard. That was before much was known about the kind of disability he had. She'd worked with Timmy when the schools wouldn't, and she'd carried on even when her husband died and she had the full burden to bear alone. Timmy couldn't have made it without her. I wondered now if she was going to be able to make it without Timmy.

"I'm so sorry," I said.

She nodded and looked into my eyes.

"I'm sorry too," she said. "But I've been around for a long time. I've had enough anger and hatred and regret for a lifetime. I was angry when Timmy was born. I was angry when his father died. If they catch the killers, Emerson, I want you to tell them something."

"I will."

"Tell them I forgive them. I won't live with anger, not any longer."

Less than thirty minutes later we again drove by the gas station, on the way back to town and to Moore Funeral Home. The Volvo was still there.

As we were wrapping things up at the funeral home with Wally, Martin asked if I had a lesson prepared for Sunday.

"Trust me," I told him. "I'll work on it tonight."

"I do trust you," Martin said. Again he made me feel a little awkward, maybe even a little guilty. Martin thought a whole lot more of me than I thought of myself, I realized. I wondered what he saw that I didn't.

What *I* saw was a reporter who wasn't much good at anything else. My goal of entering the ministry had been set aside when it seemed to me that my spiritual gift was backsliding. Martin was right; it *had* been months since I'd seen the inside of a church.

Maybe he couldn't pawn off the junior high class on anyone else. Maybe I was just convenient. But maybe he *did* trust me.

Later that evening I sat alone in my apartment leafing through a Bible. I had no idea what I'd teach the class tomorrow, but my thoughts weren't on the class anyway. I was thinking about a blue Volvo parked in front of a gas station. For a few minutes I wondered . . . About 7 P.M. I decided to stop wondering and find out. I dialed the number to Remington's apartment. I got her answering machine. I told her to call as soon as she got in. Then I grabbed my coat. I took the stairs three at a time (ignoring the warnings of the sign below at my own peril; kids, don't try this at home). I got into my car and pulled out into the night. Five minutes later I was parked at the old restaurant, wondering what to do. Something wasn't right.

The Volvo was still there, along with three or four other cars. Not a soul was visible in the gas station, but light was coming from under the closed garage doors.

I parked my car, then jogged across the empty highway about fifty yards west of the station, hopefully well out of sight. I crept up to the station slowly, hoping to get a look inside the garage. I worked my way up to the garage itself, then hit the ground and crawled up to one of the bay doors. The half-inch crack between the door and the cement was just enough to peek through.

I didn't like what I saw.

In time of need it's good to have a friend beside you. And I had a friend that I particularly needed to have beside me right then. I crawled away, sprinted back across the highway, and jumped into my car. I drove a couple of blocks back toward town, to a twenty-four-hour gas station with a pay phone.

"Come on . . . answer," I urged as the phone rang. After three of the longest rings I'd ever held my breath through, I heard a very welcome Israeli accent.

"David, it's Emerson. We've got some trouble. I need you, buddy, and I need you quick."

"What's up, Emerson . . . Where are you?"

"Meet me at the old restaurant across from Sandersen's gas

station. I think Remington might be in trouble. She's in there with probably at least six skinheads."

"I'll be there in ten minutes."

I drove back to the restaurant and waited. David arrived there three minutes early. He carried a duffel bag.

"What's in this?" I said as I started to open it.

He grabbed the bag and smiled.

"Tools," he said. "Drive up to the pumps like you want some gas. Leave the keys in the car, just in case. I'll take it from there."

"I bet you will," I said. But I complied. David was, after all, one of God's Chosen People. Considering all the Israeli nation had been through in its history, I just hoped God didn't plan on "choosing" us tonight.

I turned on my headlights as I drove into the station. I deliberately crossed the black hose that sounded a bell inside the station and garage, so they would hear my arrival. I took a breath and got out of the car.

No one was in sight. The garage was closed but bright and silent. No one was behind the counter as I entered the station. I stood at the counter and waited a moment. I rang the little bell beside the cash register.

I heard the back door of the garage open, then saw the back door to the station open. A nondescript skinhead emerged and started toward the cash register to take my money. He didn't seem excited about it. But then he stopped.

I looked into his eyes and realized that this was Benny, the punk who'd been here when we came with the police. He recognized me too.

A gun appeared in his hand, but I was still looking into his eyes.

These aren't the eyes of someone who wants to be my friend, I thought astutely.

"Ain't that a coincidence," he said. "We have your partner in the other room. We figured she was either a reporter or a cop, and she ain't no cop. Neither are you. Now follow me back out the door here and go into the garage. I've got some friends I want you to meet."

I tried not to make any sudden moves. As the skinhead started to back out the door of the station, he smiled.

"That's it — nice and slow," he said.

And then he disappeared, very sudden-like, through the door and into the blackness of the night. All I heard was a *snap*.

"Emerson!" I heard David's voice hiss from outside. "I think I broke something. I need some help. Come on!"

"Are you hurt?" I asked, moving slowly toward the back door.

"Not me . . . him," David said, coming into the light and holding the limp body of the skinhead. "I think I broke his wrist . . . his arm . . . something. Anyway, he passed out. What should I do with him?"

I guess they don't teach you *everything* in the Israeli army.

I noticed David didn't have his duffel bag. Apparently he didn't need it.

"Don't ask *me*!" I whispered in response to his question about the skinhead. "Drop him behind the counter there."

As David dragged the skinhead across the floor, I reached for the phone. I dialed 911 and left the receiver sitting on the counter. I didn't want to start any long conversations with a dispatcher — I just wanted a cop or two.

"Was that really necessary?" I asked, looking back at the unconscious skinhead, remembering that this was the one who'd taunted David.

David ignored my question. Maybe he was right; maybe it was necessary. It was at least gratifying, I guess.

"Come on!" David said. "Now we'll get Remington out of here."

He turned to me and smiled. "You like this girl, don't you?"

"Gimme a break. She's a fellow journalist," I said. And then I smiled too. "But let's not go too easy on these guys just the same."

We went out the back door and over to the rear door of the

garage. David pressed something into my hand. It was a revolver — the skinhead's when he still had the use of his arm. It was a blue-steel .38 standard police-type revolver. It felt awkward and large in my hand.

"Now this part is simple," David said. "You wait thirty seconds, then knock. Put the pistol in your jeans, at the small of your back."

"And you'll take care of the rest, right?"

"Right."

He disappeared again. A second later I heard his whisper.

"I brought my camera, Emerson. Think we can score some overtime for this?"

I didn't answer. I counted slowly — very slowly — to thirty. Then I knocked.

When the door opened I looked into the face of a very confused skinhead.

"Your friend out here says he needs a hand," I said. "He says the cash register won't open."

The skinhead peered at me suspiciously and leaned out a little, looking at someone behind me, I guess.

Unfortunately no one was behind me. That fact bothered me a little. The guy started to turn to talk to someone inside the garage.

That's when I kicked the door with every bit of strength I could muster.

It caught the skinhead square in the face. It looked like it must have hurt. He went down like the price of Texas crude in 1985. *I'm bad at this*, I thought.

I grabbed the door when it bounced back off his face, opened it the rest of the way, and let myself into the garage, stepping on my host's chest as I entered. A quick glance told me he was already bleeding.

"Good evening, gentlemen," I said to the group of four black-clad neo-Nazis gathered around a young woman. The woman was indeed Remington, but she didn't look particularly happy.

Eye makeup sure looks bad when it runs. She sat on a steel drum, looking very nervous — and very glad to see me.

But in a split second I realized she would know I wasn't the cavalry. Worse, the punks would realize that too.

"The cops are on their way, and you'd better hope they get here soon," I said to the skinheads.

They seemed frozen with surprise. The thaw was coming though.

"Frankie, get the door," one of the taller ones said. You know, these guys sure looked alike, but I was starting to learn to tell them apart. My old friend Frank, the first attendant I'd met, went to the door. The taller skinhead turned back to me.

"We'll take care of this guy," he said.

I'd never pulled a gun on anyone in my life, but I guess I was just about ready to make that commitment. The problem was, the tall guy beat me to it.

"Hands on your head," he said. "And get on your knees."

The tall guy looked a little older. He also looked a little more hardened than the others.

"You bet, boss," I said. "But you'd better check with Frankie. I don't think he's doing a good job covering the door."

The tall guy, apparently the leader, looked behind me, and I followed suit. All that could be seen was the limp body of the guy I'd nailed — Frankie was gone. I'd heard that snapping sound again, and now I knew why.

The leader's gun hand, holding a small automatic — chrome-plated, probably .22 caliber, a gun for the timid — started to quiver. He looked from me to the door, to me, to the door, then back at me again, like a neurotic tennis fan.

And then the archangel Michael sounded the seventh trumpet and the New Jerusalem descended.

At least that's what it seemed like. I heard the grind of tires on pavement, the ripping of sheet metal, and the unmistakable horn of a mid-1970s Ford Galaxy. Then my car — *my* car, not David's, mind you — came crashing through a bay door and into the garage. The door sheared off at one end and crinkled aside like aluminum foil. The high beams were on, and the horn was still blaring. As the three remaining punks turned, I could see terror in their eyes. *This is the cavalry*, I thought.

I wasn't slow to respond appropriately to the developing situation. Already on my knees, I hit the floor in that full-body slouch I practiced so often, pulled the revolver from my belt, and rolled a couple of times for good measure. I'd seen that on TV.

My car kept coming into the garage until the driver's side door was all the way in. Then David slammed that sensitive Ford Cruise-O-Matic transmission into park — as the car was moving, mind you, causing the engine to stall and doing who knows what damage to the transmission itself. Then David leapt dramatically out of the car. I stood in awe at the injury my poor, faithful Ford was suffering at the hands of this guy who used to drive tanks for a living. I didn't have much time to think about it though.

For a split second there was no sound. It was like the silence that follows the crack of the bat when the entire crowd stands in unison, straining to see the baseball as it leaves the field. You know what I mean.

The head punk, who'd turned to watch the auto assault, started to lift his arm to aim. I figured I'd better speak up and break the silence.

"Don't move a muscle, Adolph," I said. I pulled back the hammer for that satisfying *click*, just for good measure.

He spun back around, and that's when David nailed him. I didn't think Adolph would get up anytime soon.

I turned my attention and my weapon to the other two punks, who were huddling around Remington and still looking stupid.

"You guys, on the floor," I said. They complied rather quickly. Remington remained atop her barrel, looking confused.

"We're here!" I said brightly. I almost got a smile out of her.

David was up again, looking pleased with himself.

"You liked that? I did that with a Merkevah tank once," he said. "These garage doors, they're nothing. They're weak."

I didn't reply. I saw flashing blue lights sliding into the parking lot, so I lowered my gun.

Two cops, one of whom I knew, entered through the now-open bay door, winding their way around my car. Their eyes were wide, and their guns were drawn.

"What have we here?" Officer Emilio Ramirez said with a smile when he saw me. He walked over to me, and I handed him my gun as his partner started to take a body count. The other cop looked familiar. I'd seen her out on patrol, but I'd never met her.

"Don't miss the one in the station, slumped behind the counter," I said to her. "And there should be another one out back. Better get some ambulances. And you'd better call Singer. He's not going to be happy with me."

Adolph, the head punk (I didn't know what his real name was, but then I didn't care much either), was still on the ground swearing and holding his arm. The punk I'd bumped with the door was starting to groan. Remington was starting to smile. Ramirez was talking into his radio (they wear little portables these days, with a little microphone clipped to their epaulets; it's kind of cute, actually). I went over to Remington and grinned.

"Kinda theatrical, wouldn't you say?" I asked.

She smiled again.

"Not bad," she said. "About two hours later than I would have liked, but not bad."

"Are you hurt?"

"No. They didn't touch me. I told them I was an undercover cop and that the whole building was bugged. They didn't quite believe me, but they didn't quite disbelieve me either. They were scared enough to not do anything except yell at me. They were just about ready to call their boss when you two showed up. Boy, these guys are stupid."

I heard a woman's voice behind me.

"We'd like to do the questioning, if you don't mind, Dunn," the cop said. "Singer's told me about you two. He didn't say anything about this other guy though."

"How bad off are they?" I asked the officer, whose name badge read Nix. I recognized the name from some reports: Sally Nix.

"No one's dead, but two are unconscious. No surface wounds or lacerations, but several broken bones," she said. "Another one has a broken nose and probably a mild concussion. And you tore the heck out of this garage."

David was trying — in excited, somewhat broken English — to explain to Ramirez all that had happened. I think he was just confusing the poor guy because after a moment Ramirez waved me over.

"What is all this?" he asked.

"At the very least kidnapping, unlawfully carrying weapons, and terroristic threats," I said. "Probably aggravated assault as well, and if we can't find Remington's purse I say we nail them for armed robbery too."

One of the punks who hadn't said anything yet started to get up. David subtly stepped on his neck, and the skinhead went back down. Nix didn't seem to notice; she was getting Remington's story.

After a minute or two the whole parking lot was filled with flashing lights and uniforms. Paramedics set fractures and checked irises on the wounded, verbally admiring David's handiwork.

"Good clean break," one said about Adolph's arm. "Where else did you hit him? We'd better know where to check for internal bleeding."

David started pointing at various parts of the man's body, but before he could say anything none other than Detective Sergeant Bill Singer walked into the somewhat breezy garage. He was dressed in a dark suit, and he smelled good. *Oh, great*, I thought, *he was on a date.*

"I don't believe it," he said. "I don't know what's going on here, but, Emerson, I'm sure you're the cause."

"Not him," Remington said, "me. I came to check out this guy's story on Timmy's murder. When I asked too many questions, he got suspicious and called his friends. One of his friends recognized me from the raid, and they've been keeping me here — waving guns in my face all the while — since 4:30 this afternoon. Emerson and David were just trying to help me."

"Cuff them all," Singer said, motioning to the still-mobile punks. He turned to David. "What did you hit these guys with — a nightstick? Did you shoot anyone?"

"No weapons," David said. "Guns make me nervous." He smiled. Singer didn't.

"Call Sandersen . . . get him out here," Singer told one of the cops milling about. "Get the crime-scene van out here — I want photos of *everything*."

He motioned to another one of the cops.

"Line up the juvies along that wall there, get IDs, and start running their names through the computer," he said. "Take the wounded to the emergency ward, but I want two of us for each one of them. Have southside patrol send a couple of cars up."

He looked at David and me.

"You messed up," he said. "You endangered Remington's life and your own by not calling us first. And you've damaged a man's place of business. If he wants to press charges against you two, I'll bust you myself."

I nodded. It was true. The cops train for this kind of thing. If Sandersen wanted to nail us, he could.

Singer turned to Remington, who was still giving a statement to Nix.

"Did they assault you?" he asked a bit more gently.

"No," she said. "I'm fine. I told them I was a cop and that you guys would be here any minute. They were as scared as I was."

Ramirez, who'd taken my gun and now held the automatic Adolph had been waving, brought the weapons over to Singer.

"You should send that .38 to the county's ballistics lab," I said. "It might be the gun that killed Timmy. I wouldn't put it past these guys."

I was guessing, but I thought it was a good guess. The armed robbery seemed just a little too set up, and Frankie knew just a little too little. Remington's instincts were right. His skinhead friends were probably involved.

Singer grunted. He examined the weapons and saw something I hadn't thought to look for: the serial numbers had already been removed — filed off.

The next half hour was a blur of questions. The department's van arrived. A cop started taking photos, and as soon as they let him, David started doing the same. They wouldn't let me move my car until it was chalked, photographed, tagged and interrogated. Don't ask me how a car is interrogated — cops have their ways. It seemed to have suffered no obvious ill effects from crashing through a metal door, though I was still going to discuss that matter with David. When he was taking a shot of its right front wheel, now atop what was once part of the door, I walked over to him.

"Why *my* car?" I asked. "What did it ever do to you?"

"Well, I had some tools with me," David said. "I had bolt cutters, I had a hacksaw, I had a crowbar. I was going to cut the chain and raise the door, but when I saw the gun, I decided that would take too much time. And your car was convenient. Besides, I knew you wouldn't mind — it was for Remington."

I didn't reply, although I thought of several viable responses. A moment later Sandersen walked in. He looked very pale. He looked from me to Remington and then to Singer. Singer walked over, and the two started talking in low voices. I heard little. It seemed to be mostly a narrative of what had gone on all day. Sandersen was getting whiter by the second. He spoke up after I heard the words "pressing charges."

"No, no, I don't think so," he said. "I don't think we'll need to do that."

He looked at me.

"Emerson, I want to thank you for your courageous actions tonight," he said. "What happened here today was reprehensible. Ms. Remington, I want you to know that I'll be behind you in prosecuting every one of these thugs to the full extent of the law."

"But they're *your* thugs," she said. "Listen to that, boys . . . he's rolling you over — selling you out."

The skinheads, all sitting in a nice, neat little row, didn't flinch.

Sandersen turned to Singer with pleading eyes.

"When I make an investment in a business, I try to make an investment in the community as well," he said in what sounded like a very rehearsed speech. "I try to hire the unfortunate. I try to give boys like these a chance to make something of themselves. Frank, for example. He was a dropout; he could have been manager of this place in a year."

Sandersen looked around. "Where *is* Frank anyway?"

"In a cast by now," I said. "David broke him."

It was midnight when Singer finally let us leave. Sandersen had left long ago, as had most of the cops. Singer was still talking to Remington. David snapped a few last photos, waved, and crossed the highway to his Toyota. He was still a little smug about the whole evening. I didn't blame him. I was impressed too. And I was awfully glad he was on my side.

Remington stood outside and guided me as I drove my car out of the garage. The metal door to the bay was still mostly attached at one side, so it didn't fall on my hood or anything as I pulled out. I parked next to the Volvo and waited for Remington.

She and Singer emerged at the same time.

"Let's not do this again," Singer said. He didn't bother to wave as he left. One cop remained; it was Nix. She was posted there to watch the place until Sandersen could get someone out to fix that door in the morning. She wouldn't stay there all night, I knew; they'd rotate. In an hour another officer would be by to relieve her. She looked bored.

Remington walked around to her driver's-side door and started to leave.

"I owe you one, Emerson," she said. "Let me know if there's anything I can do."

I looked at my watch and smiled. "I was hoping you'd say that.

I'll pick you up at 9 in the morning. Don't wear any clothing you value."

She frowned but nodded.

"What are we going to do — knock off another gas station?"

"Trust me," I said with a smile.

Remington was still frowning when she pulled out and left. I started back toward my car.

"Dunn . . ."

I looked back at Nix.

"Take care of her," she said to me. "She's not nearly as tough as she'd like you to think. Exhaustion is first. She'll sleep tonight. The rest comes later. I've seen this a thousand times. She'll need some extra strength."

"I know."

"Do what you can."

For the third time in a week I was told that. First Bill Singer, then Martin, now some cop I'd just met. They all saw something I didn't. I got into my car — my miraculously unharmed car — and drove home. The news station was telling me about the gang wars in Houston again. I switched it off. I'd had enough for one night.

When I got home I avoided my Bible. I'd just have to wing it in the morning. Martin has a set of what he calls his "breadbox sermons" — good for when he's asked to speak at another church or when something's come up and he just hasn't had time to study. I'd heard all of them three or four times at least. Some I could repeat in my sleep. My dog says I sometimes do.

I had the same sorts of studies I knew by heart from my Sunday school teaching days.

I slept until 8 A.M. when my alarm went off. A quick bagel and shower later, I was driving across town to the southwest side, where the junior college sat. Remington lived in one of several mediocre complexes there. This specific complex catered to the several hundred nursing students from the college (the only really strong academic program there) and was therefore occupied mostly by women. They had a security guard, and most people knew their neighbors. Remington said she felt a little safer there.

I neared her apartment building with a mixture of emotions in my throat. I'd only been here once, a few months ago when I'd dropped her off after a city council meeting. Her car had died in the parking lot of City Hall (Daddy had AAA out before morning). I wasn't sure I'd recognize her apartment now, but luckily she was looking for me. She stuck her head out the door of a second-floor unit and called down to me.

I parked and went up. Her apartment was smaller than mine, believe it or not. It was almost an efficiency, but it did have a separate kitchen and living room. It had one bedroom, but the door was closed. She had some nice furniture — early 1980s, I estimated. Poofy couches with saddlebag backs and a brass-and-glass table. Either her mother or her father had redecorated fairly recently, I guessed. I myself preferred to get my furniture from garage sales.

The only striking aspect of her apartment was the bookcase. It took up a whole wall; it must have been ten feet long and was less than six inches from the ceiling. And it was filled. I liked that. She — or someone — must have brought in the lumber and built it right there.

"Is this OK?" she asked about her outfit — a sweatshirt and jeans.

Herein is a point I feel must be made. Every girl I'd ever dated had at one time or another asked my advice about clothing: "Is this OK?" or "What should I wear?" And without exception each girl on each occasion completely ignored my advice. I'm all for that, of course, since I wasn't quite a fashion-plate myself — that is, according to the same girls, each of whom also at one point or another made significant changes to my wardrobe. But the point is, why did they bother to ask? But that's a completely different mystery.

"Fine," I said. "Bring a dress too."

She started to frown again.

"Trust me," I said. "Remember, you owe me a favor."

I wasn't above using guilt when it suited my purposes.

She went into the bedroom. I caught a glimpse of it when she opened the door, and I realized why she'd had it closed. The room looked about like mine. Her stack of dirty clothes was virtually indistinguishable from mine, except it was mostly pastels.

I don't own any pastels, despite the sincere efforts of several aforementioned girlfriends.

I smiled victoriously.

Remington emerged with a warm-looking, dark green dress and some black pumps in her hand.

"Great," I said. "Let's go."

"Where?"

"Church."

I was already out of the apartment before I realized she wasn't following. I turned back.

"What's wrong?"

"First of all, I haven't been to church in years, and secondly, I didn't figure you for the church type," she said in a sort of panicky voice. "No way."

"I need you, Remington," I said. "Timmy's mother teaches a Sunday school class, and we have to take over for a couple of weeks."

She cringed. The part about Timmy's mother had her. Like I said, guilt. But judge me not — I was desperate.

"OK, but let's not make a big deal about it," she said. "This isn't going to be anything weird, is it?"

I laughed. "No . . . pretty tame as a matter of fact. It won't hurt a bit. Now come on."

She still refused to go to church in jeans, despite the impending terrors of the junior high class I warned her about. She put on the dress, pulled her hair back, and got a long, black wool coat. She actually looked very nice.

We drove most of the way to the church without saying a word. Something was wrong. I felt a little tug at the back of my soul; I felt uncomfortable but wasn't sure why. Then it hit me. I was bothered by something Remington had said.

"What did you mean you hadn't figured me for the church type?" I said.

"Oh, don't get mad at that," she said. "I just didn't know you were the kind that went for that sort of thing."

I let it go, but it still bothered me.

We drove up to the church at about 9:30. We walked into the foyer and around to the right until we found the right classroom. I could tell it was the right classroom by the noise. Sunday school started at about 9:45, and we were fifteen minutes early, but the class was already starting to fill. We went in, and the kids calmed down a little — but not much.

I don't know why, but the room itself was blue. The old wood paneling, the baseboards, and even the windowsills were bright sky-blue. There were a few mass-produced paintings of a very American-looking Jesus on the walls. In one painting He was calling into a cave — Lazarus' grave, I presumed; in another He was leading a bunch of children and sheep around.

I had a quick revelation that chances are Jesus looked a lot more like David than like me.

I walked up to the lectern and surveyed my charges — ten or twelve cherubic junior high kids.

Junior high is that magical age when a young person most deserves to be sold to the Gypsies.

I'd taught this class before — probably more than a year ago, one Sunday when Anna was sick. Timmy still came to help with discipline, though. I looked at Remington, who still stood at the door. She looked a little overwhelmed.

A wadded piece of construction paper flew by my ear. *Never take your eyes off these guys*, I reminded myself.

The class was almost quiet by now. Or at least it was down to an almost-acceptable level. I still recognized some of the faces.

"Dennis, get these guys quiet for me, will you?" I asked.

A freckled, stout boy of about thirteen punched the boy beside him, then put his fingers in his mouth and whistled.

"Thank you," I said. "Most of you guys and girls know me. My name is Emerson, and I'll be your substitute for a few weeks. This is Ms. Remington."

She smiled at the kids, and they smiled back. So far, so good.

She took a seat at the back of the classroom to await further orders.

"OK, kids, get your Bibles out," I said.

I smiled at the kids. They smiled back, but they didn't move. Not a muscle.

"What's wrong?"

"We use the Sunday school book," Dennis said as if I was missing something. "This is Sunday school. The Bible's for church. Here we're on Lesson 49. We only have three lessons to go."

He handed me a booklet that looked exactly like what you'd expect adults to produce for junior high students. It had comics, crossword puzzles, and a single Bible verse hidden in today's lesson somewhere.

"Dennis, open that window," I said.

As he did so, I frisbeed the booklet right out. Dennis and the other kids stared after the departed item.

"Grown-ups," I said. "Gimme a break. Now get your Bibles out."

This time they complied. Remington looked a little confused, but she was willing to go along. She didn't have much choice.

The lesson was a simple one; everything needed for it was found in the book of Habakkuk. No comics were included either. It went pretty well. We got through the first two chapters quickly; it wasn't complicated stuff.

"So what's the point?" I asked.

A girl I knew was named Samantha raised her hand.

"That bad things do happen sometimes, but that doesn't mean God isn't at work?" she asked.

"Yup. When Habakkuk says, 'Therefore the law is slacked, and judgment doth never go forth: for the wicked doth encompass about the righteous; therefore wrong judgment proceedeth,' he's saying that it looks like the bad guys won," I said. "But then God says, 'Don't you worry about the bad guys — there are worse ones that are about to take care of them. And then I'll take care of the worse guys.'"

I knew the kids could understand what I was saying, and I think junior high students are probably the ones who need to hear that message the most. Every school has a bully, every kid's been accused of something he or she hasn't done, and every child wants to know why adults can be so unfair. A child's faith can be shaken by something as simple as a bloody nose or as complicated as a divorce.

I went on to the final three verses of the book, some of the most soul-searing in the entire Bible. "'Although the fig tree shall not blossom, neither shall the fruit be on the vines; the labor of the olive shall fail, and the fields shall yield no meat; the flock shall be cut off from the fold, and there shall be no cattle in the stalls: yet I will rejoice in the Lord, I will joy in the God of my salvation. The Lord God is my strength.'"

"Even when bad stuff happens, we have to be happy about it?" Dennis asked.

"No, you don't," I said. "He doesn't say anything about being happy with all that. And look, Habakkuk even got away with questioning God. He didn't get toasted for it. God understands that sometimes we don't understand; He just wants us to trust Him. The important thing is that He's forgiven us and we're His for good. No matter what bad things happen, we can count on that. Even when things look bad, that's something to take some comfort in."

It didn't look like I'd changed any lives, but some of the kids seemed a little quieter when the bell rang and they started filing out the door. Maybe I'd gotten them thinking anyway.

"Not bad," Remington said. "You didn't need me a bit. They listened to every word you said."

"Yeah. Must be an off week for them," I said. "Usually they're pretty wild."

Remington wanted to "freshen up," so I walked her down the hall, then loitered for a few minutes as she got ready. When she came out, with her hair down now, I tried not to notice that she was gorgeous. After all, this was church.

The halls had filled with kids running to and fro (I prefer to see them run a bit more fro than to, myself) and with church members standing around socializing. I led Remington back up the hallway to the foyer. Martin was standing in the middle of it, greeting people. I tried to slip Remington and myself by unnoticed. I was nearly successful too. Then I felt a hand grasp my khaki pants at knee-level.

I looked down into two of the most beautiful green eyes imaginable. Susie reached up, and I bent to pick her up.

"Dangerous Sue," I said, lifting a child who was about 50 percent bigger than I'd expected her to be; I guess it *had* been months since I'd been here. Susie's blonde curls were straightening now, and her face wasn't as cheeky. The dimples were still there, but she was now a child and definitely not a baby.

"She's missed you," Martin said. "Are you and your guest coming over for lunch? *We've* missed you too."

I looked at Remington. Her eyes didn't exactly say yes, but they didn't say no either. I bet she had a freezer full of burritos waiting for her at home too.

"Sure," I said. "We'd love to. Martin, this is Remington."

She nudged me.

"Aggie, I mean," I amended.

She nudged me again. I gave up.

"Just call me A. C.," she said, taking Martin's hand. Martin was smiling that pastor's smile again.

"I love reading your articles," Martin said. "You give our boy here a run for his money."

The quickest way to a reporter's heart is flattery.

Remington smiled.

I gave Susie one last squeeze and set her down. She saw another best friend coming in, and a split second later I was forgotten. Dames. I led Remington into the sanctuary.

We found a seat near the door. That's what they teach you in journalism school. Sit near the door; you can get out quicker.

That is especially advantageous when city council members start throwing things.

As we sat down, Remington looked nervous.

"It's been a while, Emerson," she said. "Probably five or six years. And even then I only went a couple of times a year. You know, Easter and Christmas Eve."

"It's been a few months for me," I said. "Don't worry about it. If you don't know the songs, fake it. I always do."

She smiled and brushed some hair away from her face.

A few of the wreaths from Timmy's funeral still graced the sanctuary. The black looked out of place with the Christmas decorations that were starting to emerge: the holly above the tall stained-glass windows behind the pulpit and above the baptistery (where Martin got to wear his fishing waders and dunk new members — he liked that) and the garland across the backs of the wooden pews.

Remington made it through the grueling stand/sit portion of the service, the part that has been known to scare visitors off by the hundreds. You know, you go into a church and you never know what's going on. Some congregations stand for prayers, some of them sit for prayers; some stand to sing, some sit to sing; some even stand up and sit down for no reason whatsoever. Remington followed my lead on that. On the singing she did OK by herself. She had a good ear for music and picked up most of the songs by the second or third verse. We were just a few days away from Christmas, so a couple of the songs were carols she knew already.

The sermon was about par for Martin; that is to say, you came away thinking. No fire, no brimstone, just lots of food for thought. He was leading up to Christmas, and this Sunday he spoke about how much faith it must have taken on Joseph's part to stay engaged to this pregnant woman, Mary. Even before the angel came and explained the deal to him, he stuck by her. According to Jewish law, he had every right to break the engagement, but he didn't.

Martin rarely speculates. He says there's enough in the Bible already without us adding our two cents' worth. But this time he did just a little conjecturing, offering a possible motive for Joseph.

"He forgave her," Martin said. "She was pregnant, and until the dream he had no way of knowing that was the Lord's doing. He must have naturally assumed Mary had been unfaithful. But he forgave her."

That was the gist of it. I could see that. So Joseph must have been a great guy. But something in all that stayed with me as a little nagging voice I'd have to work to ignore.

After the service we left quickly. I paused just long enough to tell Meg, Martin's wife, that he'd invited us to lunch. She wasn't surprised or displeased; she never was. I told her we'd meet them at their house.

A few people made it a point to say hello to me; a few looked a little surprised to see me. I think that bothered me a little too. But we ducked out successfully and got into my car.

"They live a few blocks from here," I said. "Meg will be in as soon as she rounds up the kids. Martin will be home a little later — he always sticks around to talk to everyone."

We drove over to their place and pulled into the classic suburban driveway. The red brick house looked warm and familiar.

Martin had planted some oaks — and even some pecan trees last year. I had helped. They looked secure now — strong and hardy. By the time Susie was ready for high school they'd be almost stately.

We got out of the car and walked across the brown lawn to the porch. I reached under the swing, found the key clinging to the magnet, and let us into the house. Remington looked a little uncomfortable.

"You do this often?" Remington asked.

"Not really," I said. "Not in a while either. But I know the routine. Come on — it's our job to set the table."

We went into the living room, and I paused. Their Christmas

tree was up. I hadn't even thought about putting one up at my apartment, but the sight suddenly made me wonder why I hadn't. The lights were plugged into the socket below the front picture window. I hit the switch on the wall, and the tree lit up. Remington put her hand on my back, and we just stared at it for a moment.

I was handing Remington some plates from the cabinet when we heard Meg and the kids come in. Sandra was six, Ricky five, and Susie three. All three had Martin's blond hair, but most of the resemblance stopped there.

In addition, they were three very different children. Sandra, the oldest, was very concerned with keeping the other two in line. She was pretty, prim, and proper — and in fact very elegant for a six-year-old. If she invited you to a tea party, your pinky had better be raised, and your elbows had better keep off the table.

Ricky was the kind of boy who just enjoyed being a boy. He liked climbing trees, chasing bugs, and watching cowboys. More importantly, this kid loved my sailboat. Last summer I taught him how to trim the jib sail when we tacked and jibed (that's boat-talk for turning); after fifteen minutes of instruction he was one of the best crews I've ever sailed with. He wasn't really strong enough to pull the sheets (ropes to you landlubbers out there) tight, but he got the sail around to the leeward side of the boat when I needed it there. If the sheet needed an extra tug a few moments later, I was happy to oblige.

And Susie was Susie. Enough said.

Meg entered the kitchen and seemed not at all surprised about a backslidden reporter and some girl she'd never met setting her table. Meg had dark hair, green eyes, and cheekbones most women would kill for. Her smile was as warm as her kitchen.

"Good to have you back, guy," she said. "This must be A. C. I see Emerson has already put you to work. That's really *his* job. Your first time here, you're supposed to be treated like company."

"I don't mind," Remington said with a smile, taking some plates across to the table in the connected dining room. "You have a lovely house."

They went on like that for some time. Meg asked polite questions about Remington, and Remington made polite compliments about everything. I politely excused myself once the table was set and the roast was heating up. I'd go find Ricky. I didn't have to put up with too much politeness out of him.

The kid was out back despite the chilling breeze that had picked up. The backyard was brown and had about the same number of young trees as the front yard, but it also had a small garden, now lying dormant. Ricky was just beyond that, at a small tree which had a bird feeder hanging from it.

"I want to invent something," he told me as if we were picking up a conversation we'd left off just yesterday. "Something for the bird feeder."

"What?"

"Something to keep the blue jays out but lets the cardinals and sparrows in," he said. "The blue jays chase the others away. Last year we saw a blue jay kill a baby squirrel. He pecked it."

I considered the problem.

"Which are bigger, Ricky — blue jays or sparrows?"

"Blue jays," he said with confidence. This boy knew his birds. "They're big. They're fat too, from all the birdseed they hog. Hey, maybe I could build a door."

"A door to the bird feeder that blue jays couldn't get through but the others could?"

He nodded. "I'll think on it," he said. And I knew he would.

We talked a little more before we went in for lunch. Ricky told me about kindergarten, about having to take naps, and about getting a little bored because he already knew his letters and numbers. But he had lots of friends there, he said, so it wasn't too bad. First grade would be better, he assured me, because then you get to start reading. He was looking forward to that.

"Will you read my newspaper?" I asked.

He grinned. "Maybe."

That response, I felt, called for immediate action, so I tackled the kid, but within seconds he had me.

Maybe I ought to get him and David together, I thought to myself through the searing pain and agony as I was given the Super Diabolical Power Crusher Hold. Had Meg not called us in for lunch right at that moment, I might not be here now.

"Coming," we yelled in unison.

"When can we sail again?" Ricky asked.

"The lake won't be warm enough until sometime in March," I answered. "Seems like a long time, doesn't it?"

"Yeah," he said.

We went back into the house. Martin, home by now, was sitting at the breakfast bar looking into the kitchen at his wife and Remington, who was pouring gravy into a duck-shaped gravy boat. A duck-shaped gravy boat? I knew that neither ducks nor boats have anything whatsoever to do with gravy, but I let it pass. It's best not to get too worked up over these sorts of things.

Ricky ran into the bathroom to wash up. I figured I'd wait my turn. I joined Martin at the breakfast bar.

"How did class go?" he asked me.

"Fine," I said. "No problems. I think the kids were all well-behaved because Remington was there with me."

"Or maybe it was because you chucked the Sunday school book out the window," Meg suggested. "About time someone did that."

Martin laughed.

"I knew you could handle it," he said. Then the tone of his voice changed — to the Voice that comes with the Pastor's

Concerned Frown (which works on the same principle as the Smile).

"A. C. was just telling us about your little adventure last night. Very impressive."

I didn't respond. I wasn't sure how I should.

"Sounds like a very dangerous situation," he added.

"Is that a reproach?" I asked. "If so, I guess I deserve it. I should have called the police in the first place, I know."

"Why didn't you?"

I stalled.

"I don't really know. Maybe because I think this is *my* fight now. It's gone beyond just a few burglaries. Timmy was killed, and Remington . . . Well, I knew David and I could take care of it."

Remington turned away and started fussing with the dinner rolls.

"There's more," Martin says.

"Yeah," I said after a moment. "I think I'm a little disappointed in the police. I don't think I can trust them on this one. I have no proof, but I think there's a connection between the gun store break-in, the burglaries, and Timmy's death. And if there is a connection, the cops sure aren't looking for it. They're too busy planning Mike Sandersen's campaign for city council."

"So you took on a gang?"

"I didn't do it alone," I said. "I had the Israeli army with me. David did *most* of the hard work, anyway."

In spite of himself, Martin grinned. "No turning the other cheek for this Jew, eh?"

I smiled too. "I gave him a New Testament once," I said. "I guess he hasn't gotten to that part yet."

Ricky, Sandra, and Susie entered the dining room from various other parts of the house, ready to eat.

As usual, the meal was good. Most of the table conversation centered on Remington. The kids seemed to like her. Then Martin asked her what she thought about his sermon, and everything got *polite* again. It was as if the depth of the conversation was suddenly broken up by shoals and we were all steering our boats as carefully as we could to avoid scraping the rocks. The meal ended with a wonderful dessert, but the now-useless conversation left me with kind of an empty feeling. I could tell that Remington wasn't as comfortable as she had been a few minutes earlier.

The kids finished up, then went back to whatever they were doing before lunch. Apparently they had better things to do than spend quality time with us adults. Can't say I blamed them much.

Martin got up, plugged in the coffeepot, and asked me to follow him out into the study he'd converted his garage into. A glance at Remington told me she'd be fine. Meg was already starting to warm her up again.

"Leave the dishes, honey," Martin said to Meg. "Emerson will get those later."

Martin's book-lined study was small. But then, he didn't need much space. He had a desk, his computer, and about a jillion volumes of theological works. I'd read a lot of them, but only a fraction of the total.

"You did well today," he said, sitting at his desk and turning his chair to face me. "And you did a good job with the funeral arrangements."

I unfolded the only other chair in the room and sat down. "Thanks."

"She's a nice girl, Emerson."

I didn't like his tone.

"What are you getting at?" I asked.

"It's about time for you to shape up, Emerson," he said with a little less patience in his voice. "I've given you almost a year now. You're angry, and you've got to do something about it."

I didn't say anything.

"She's gone from your life," he went on, "but you're still alive. The world didn't end. And here you are with an attractive girl just as smart and just as charming."

"You're wrong," I said. "I'm not angry. I'm not mad at anyone . . . Particularly Julie . . . That would take effort . . . And I've expended all the effort I'm going to on her."

"You're still not getting it," he said. "It's not Julie you're taking this out on. It's God."

Again I didn't say anything. I've found that if you wait long enough, something usually comes up and you won't *have* to say anything. In this case it was a knock on the study door. Sandra entered carrying two mugs of coffee.

"Thank you, princess," Martin said as she left.

He looked back at me.

"Forgive, Emerson. That's all you've got to do."

"Forgive Julie? I did that long ago."

"No . . . Forgive God. You're still blaming Him that it didn't work out."

"Well now, that's a new one," I said. "Interesting angle. I should forgive God . . . hmmm. They teach you this stuff in seminary?"

Martin sighed, and I immediately wished I hadn't said that. Martin put up with a lot from me. Maybe I *was* still angry.

"Think it over, Emerson," he said. "You'll see it. I have faith in you. Now about her . . ."

"She's just vocational competition, Martin, that's all."

"She's more than that. She's hurting. Her eyes teared up during my sermon. My guess is, she's been divorced."

"Close," I said. "Her parents were. She's still mad at her father, I think. She's only started opening up to me in the past week or so. I've known her for almost a year now and I still don't know her middle name."

Martin nodded and took a sip of coffee.

"And she also broke off an engagement," I said, remembering what Sharon had told me. "I don't know any details.

He nodded again.

"So I should do what I can, right?" I asked.

He just smiled.

It was after 3 P.M. when we left. Driving toward Remington's apartment, she asked if I would need her again the next week.

"Do you mind?" I asked. "I can get by if you're not comfortable there."

"I was comfortable," she said. "It's a pretty church. And Martin and Meg are good people. I had a nice day — one of the nicest I've had in a long time. Did you?"

"It wasn't bad."

"Meg was right," she said.

"What?"

"You don't talk to me, Emerson. You don't talk to anyone."

"Of course I do."

"But you don't tell them anything," she said. "I've just spent six hours learning about a completely different side of you. Yesterday if you'd have asked me I'd have laughed at the idea of Emerson Dunn going to church and eating lunch with the preacher and rolling around in the backyard with the preacher's kids. Meg said you weren't always like this. She said you used to be more open."

I looked down at my speedometer; I was doing 50 in a 35 mph zone. I eased off the gas pedal some.

"What happened, Emerson?"

This conversation had taken a turn for the serious, and I wasn't enjoying it.

"I don't know what you mean," I said. "Besides, you're not Miss Open Book yourself. I don't even know your middle name."

"Catherine."

"Yeah? That's not so bad. Why don't you use that instead of your initials?"

"It's my mother's name; it would have gotten too confusing."

I nodded.

"Where are we going?" she asked.

"I'm taking you home, aren't I?"

"I guess so," she said.

Dames. Now I wasn't born yesterday. I knew what her response was — a definite "I'm open for suggestions" sort of response. But this was Remington, my competition, a fellow reporter. What would we do — kick off our shoes and discuss grammar? *This kind of thing just doesn't work,* I told myself.

We drove into her complex, and I pulled into a parking space near the stairs to her apartment. I paused. So did she. It was a long five seconds.

"Good-bye," she said. "Thanks. I had a nice time."

"See you Tuesday at council," I said.

I knew I'd just blown something, but I wasn't sure what. I drove home listening to the news. Houston was getting ready for Christmas, but the gang violence seemed to be unaffected by the holiday spirit. More drive-by shootings. Doesn't anybody get out of their car for *anything* these days?

I arrived at my apartment and went on up. Once inside I saw the red light flashing at me, telling me that someone had called. I didn't think I owed anybody money, so I hit the button and listened.

The first message was from my mother. The second was from someone I did owe money to — specifically, my landlord. *He can wait until after my traditional Sunday nap,* I thought to myself. I hit the couch and instantaneously drifted off to sleep.

It was nearly dark when I awoke. The telephone was ringing. I must have been pretty dead because I'd only heard it ring once when the answering machine switched on. That means I'd slept through three rings.

"Emerson, this is Remington. Please call me."

I grabbed for the phone and hit the switch.

"I'm here," I said. "What's up?"

"There are no reports, Emerson."

"No reports about what?"

"Last night . . . Yesterday . . . The gas station."

I was suddenly very much awake.

"Did you go down to the police station looking for them? There were a bunch of cops . . . There should be a bunch of reports."

"Yes, there should be," she said. "But there's nothing."

"So what does that mean?"

"It means you were right," she said. "We can't trust the cops. They're on his side."

"Are you at home?"

"Yes."

"Stay there. I'll be over in ten minutes."

Eight minutes later I was pulling into the parking space I'd left about three hours earlier. I bounded up the stairs two at a time. I had no idea why I was in a hurry. I think it was something in her voice, or maybe something in Nix's voice last night. I didn't think Remington wanted to be alone.

She answered at the first knock. She was still wearing the green dress, but the apartment was a little neater.

"I think you're probably just getting a little worked up over nothing," I said. "Chances are the reports are sitting on Singer's desk, waiting for him to read through them in the morning. I'll call him first thing and find out."

"Don't bother," she said. "He called here earlier."

There was something about her eyes; she'd been crying again.

"Tell me," I said.

"They want to drop the case," she said. "Singer told me they have enough against me, you, and David for us to go to jail just as fast as the skinheads. I lied to Benny when I was trying to get information, and Frank plans to testify that I came on to him. You guys assaulted four or five of the skinheads and really tore up the garage. Singer says there's at least five thousand dollars' worth of damage."

She paused for a moment. "And Sandersen wants to make it up to me."

I touched her face. The eye makeup was starting to run again. "Money?" I asked.

She nodded.

I didn't know what to say. I had thought I knew Bill Singer. I didn't think he'd turn out to be a dirty cop, the kind who would use cheap intimidation tactics. He was clearly in on it; and what's more, he was dumber than I thought. Lying and "coming on" to someone aren't exactly examples of nice behavior, but there's no law against them yet. And there's no way we did five thousand dollars' worth of damage to that building. Singer was trying to scare her, and Sandersen was trying to buy her. Chances are David and I would receive similar phone calls before morning.

"But there's more," she said.

"What?"

She smiled, lifted my hand from her face, and put something in it.

A cassette tape.

Like I've always said, you've gotta respect a high-tech gal.

Many reporters, including me, record our incoming calls, in case they're tips or threats. Good reporters get quite a few of both. I was glad to see that Remington recorded her calls as well.

I grinned at her. "Let's nail 'em."

I was right — Singer called me later that night. He didn't mention money, but he said the department felt the charges against the skinheads should be dropped — and the "charges" against David and I along with them. I acted a little scared and agreed very quickly that since "no real damage was done" and no one was hurt — at least no one important — we might as well forget the whole matter. I told Singer that he probably saved my job since Andrews wouldn't look too favorably on the little excursion. Singer told me the whole thing would be our little secret. He told me to give the same message to David.

"And what are you going to do?" I asked. "Are you the type to forget this kind of thing?"

He paused just a little too long before he responded, perhaps trying to decide exactly what to say to me.

"Sure, I can forget this sort of thing," he finally said, "after a little booze, a couple of cigarettes, and some pistol range practice. Think about it."

Then he hung up.

Exactly a week later David and I were back at the old restaurant on Highway 6, taking some long-distance photos. This time the subject was a very normal-looking gasoline purchase. A blue Volvo pulled up to the pumps. A young woman got out and filled her tank with unleaded. She walked into the station, put her purse on the counter, then went back to her car for a moment, as if she'd left her checkbook on the passenger's seat. She walked back in, picked up her purse, and left.

We met her at my apartment five minutes later.

"Get it?" I asked.

She showed me a white envelope that had somehow gotten into her purse. I didn't count the money in it, but it sure *felt* like ten thousand dollars.

"Get this to the bank, open up a special savings account, and then forget about it," I told her. "Don't touch it. Someday it will be evidence."

It had been an interesting week. Mr. Andrews had suddenly warmed up to me again; apparently Sandersen had let up on him at Rotary Club. I'd spent almost every evening with Remington. I felt I was starting to get to know her. She'd told me a little about her childhood, her parents' divorce, and her stepbrother. I told her about my dog.

Christmas was a few days away, and I knew it was time to lay low. Sharon made a few comments about the various Remington sightings she'd gotten reports about. I brushed them off. Steve was scrounging for story ideas since the schools were closed for the holidays, so Barney and I had him doing the multitude of Christmas charity stories that have to be done every year. On Saturday Remington helped me pick out a food processor for my mother.

The punks were still running the gas station, but more often than not the station was closed. A sign on the pumps simply said, "Out Of Order."

I still went by the police station every day, but I avoided Bill Singer. I just went to the patrol desk, leafed through the reports, and left as soon as I had what I needed. I usually found Captain Clark watching me. When I'd see him, I'd smile as if everything was just peachy.

Sunday school continued to be a breeze. Remington was starting to add things to the discussion. Every once in a while she'd forget she was a bouncer and not a student, and she'd ask a question or two. We didn't have lunch with Martin again, although we were invited. We had a money drop to attend to, I told Martin. He raised his eyebrows but trusted me. I don't know why.

The next day a call came for me at my desk. It was Captain Clark.

"Are you free for lunch?" he asked.

"Sure," I said slowly, "but I pick the place."

"Fine," Clark said.

At noon I pulled into Walter and Gunther's parking lot. Sandersen and Clark, in Clark's white unmarked official vehicle, were close behind me. I wanted this little meeting to be on my own territory, and Clark and Sandersen didn't seem to mind. They followed me into the restaurant.

Walter looked a little suspicious. He could tell I wasn't at all comfortable. He acted as if he didn't know me from Adam, but I could tell he was keeping a close eye and ear on our booth.

"This conversation is informal, right?" Sandersen asked. He and Clark sat across from me, watching my reactions. I could tell that this was a weird kind of test. "It's off the record, isn't it?"

I cringed inwardly. I nodded and said good-bye to any hopes I had of getting any usable evidence during this little get-together. Off the record is off the record. That's the way it has to be.

"Say it," he said. He didn't trust me. And obviously there was a tape recorder somewhere. Clark was probably wired, and Sandersen's suit was too nicely pressed.

"It's off the record," I said.

He smiled and lifted the lapel of his suit jacket and reached into the inside pocket. I didn't see a wire. Instead I saw three large cigars — they looked like the expensive kind. Sandersen slowly removed one, found a cigar clipper and a lighter in his pants pocket, and fired the cigar up. I could sense Walter frowning. "Smoking dulls the taste buds," he told me once. How can someone experience the ecstasy of Walter's cooking with no taste buds? But I didn't mind the cigar. It meant Sandersen planned to sit and talk for a while, which was fine by me.

"You don't seem to like me, Emerson," Sandersen said.

"That's probably because I just don't know you," I said. "Tell me a little about yourself."

"What's to tell? I'm just a businessman who's trying to make things a little better. You're trying to make things a little better too, and I respect you for that. And I like your writing."

Like I said before, the quickest way to a reporter's heart is to compliment their writing abilities. We all have monstrous egos. But I wasn't warming up to this guy yet.

Clark spoke up.

"Emerson, we want to be able to work with you — we want you to play ball," he said. "We all have a lot at stake here. With Mike on the city council we could make a big difference in this city."

"I never was much of a ballplayer," I said. "But out of curiosity, what did you have in mind?"

"Lighten up," Clark said. "That's all; just lighten up. You can do that, can't you?"

Sandersen glanced at Clark, then spoke up. "We want the same things for this city, don't we?" he asked. "I think we do. We can work together, but you've got to overcome that antagonistic attitude of yours."

"What antagonistic attitude?"

They were silent. If they wanted me to play ball, I figured it was time for me to steal home.

"Maybe we do want the same things," I said. "I'm a little tired of the *impurity* around here."

Sandersen studied my eyes. I had used a sort of code word; "impurity" has special connotations to racists.

"We are too," he said.

"What's good for the cause is good for the city, right?" I asked.

"Right." He was still watching my eyes.

"And what about you, Ed?" I said, turning.

"We can bring back some law and order," Clark said. I couldn't believe it — he was buying it.

"We've got to teach some of the factions around here that we won't put up with their kind of troublemaking," I continued. "It's just a restoration of order — the proper order."

I caught a glimpse of Walter, who was a few tables away, listening intently. He was glaring. He knew this kind of talk inside and out, and he detested it.

I turned back to Sandersen. He was starting to buy it as well.

Like I said, given the chance people will talk. For another half hour I listened as Sandersen preached; of course, he thought he was addressing the choir. He talked about his days in college — he said he'd been at a large California university during the 1960s and got tired of being blamed for everything bad ever done to any minority simply because he was white and male. He talked about the jobs he didn't get because he was white; those blacks they hired instead must have been quota-fillers, he said. By the time success finally came — i.e., when his father died and left him enough money to embark on an investing career — he was ruthless. He'd refused to hire any of "those others" in the businesses he bought and often he fired those who were already there. He kept the government watchdogs away by hiring former juvenile delinquents, dropouts, and paroled convicts — as long as they were white, of course. And he found a loose band of skinheads in Houston — they tried to convince themselves they were a gang — that he could take under his wing.

"Sometimes they get a little out of hand," he said. "But all in all they're good kids. They should have called me that Saturday, but they were scared — just scared kids. And what that Jew did to them was unnecessary."

Walter got up and visibly — but not audibly — stormed from the room. Luckily Sandersen and Clark had their backs to him. Walter liked David an awful lot, and Walter, like most Germans, had little patience for anyone who considers himself a member of some "Master Race." He and his country had had quite enough of that.

"Yeah, well, hiring quotas," I said.

Sandersen nodded.

"I'm glad we had this talk, Emerson," he said. "You're alright. I think this can work out very profitably for all of us."

"No, I don't think so," I said. "You see, I lied. We didn't hire David because he's a minority. We hired him because he's better than any of the other photographers who applied — all of them were white, by the way. And, Sandersen, he's my best friend. I'm not playing ball with you."

I paused. They both frowned.

"You made my boys very angry," Sandersen said slowly. "I have told them to let things be, but you know how impulsive boys can be. I don't know if I can control them."

"Do your best for me, will you, Mike?" I said as I stood to leave. I caught another glimpse of Walter. He was smiling at me.

As I walked out the door, I realized that I'd left them with the check. Victory is sweet, isn't it? But that was my only victory. I knew I couldn't use the conversation we'd just had against Sandersen. I held those magical words "off the record" as sacred, and I wouldn't violate that.

However, I realized that I myself might be violated soon. Sandersen was unhappy with me, Clark was even less happy with me, and there were a few skinheads around who'd like to avenge themselves on my face, I was sure.

But hey, it was almost Christmas. I even started humming a carol as I drove back to the office.

A few days later I found myself driving to Dallas alone, wishing I wasn't. Mom loved her food processor, I loved the flannel shirts she got me, and I spent some quality time with my dog, Airborne Ranger. I was getting a little worried though. My dad was really starting to get attached to the mutt. I decided I'd better find a place with a yard soon.

I called Remington on Christmas day. She was at her mother's in Houston; she'd given me the number.

"When are you coming home?" she asked.

"Later tonight," I said. "I need to be in the office first thing in the morning. But it should be an easy week; nothing happens in between Christmas and New Year's Day."

"Call me when you get home."

"It's going to be late," I warned. "Probably about 1 A.M. or so."

"That's OK — I won't mind."

Remington didn't seem to be suffering any ill effects from her little adventure with the skinheads. Maybe Nix was wrong, I thought.

The drive home was long and lonely.

24

I called Remington when I got in. She was back at her apartment too. I'd left a little early, so it was only about 10 P.M. Still, she sounded tired, so I didn't invite myself over like I found myself wanting to. I was a little tired myself. We talked for a while, she told me about her brief visit with her dad ("they bought my stepbrother more black clothes, and Dad's new wife wouldn't leave me alone with Dad the whole time"). I told her not to worry about it, just get some sleep.

The next morning I drove to the office in a fairly good mood. Things were starting to add up. I had some definite suspicions.

"Morning, Stevie," I said as I walked in. We were the only ones who had made it in yet, except for Sharon. She was *always* there on time.

I looked over at Steve.

"How'd you make out?" I asked.

"What?" he asked.

"Your loot," I said. "What did you get?"

"Oh," he said. "Shirts. Mostly shirts."

"Yeah, me too. That's about all you get from here on out," I said. "It's kind of an adult thing. And when you get really old, you get ties."

"That's a nice tie, Mr. Andrews," Sharon said as our publisher walked in. "Is that new?"

He grumbled, and I looked at Steve and wiggled my eyebrows.

But Steve hadn't been completely honest with me. On his desk sat a new silver business card holder — hey, he'd only had business cards for a month or so.

"That's nice," I said, pointing. "Mom and Dad?"

Steve reached for it as if I were threatening to steal it and pawn it. He moved it to the other side of his desk, out of my line of sight.

"No . . . a friend," he said.

Sharon shot me a "I guess he told you what's what" look. I grinned back at her.

"Steve, have you got any stories lined up for Sunday's issue?" I asked.

"I'm doing a follow-up on Mike Sandersen's campaign," he said. "I'll take a look at who his likely opponents are going to be. He's the first one to announce, you know."

"I *do* know," I said. "That's my beat."

"Mr. Andrews asked me to do it," he said.

"That's fine. I'm not offended," I said lightly, and I meant it. I suspected Sandersen was going to want to keep his distance from me. I had figured this was going to happen.

"Good," Steve said, sounding a little more bold than he usually did, "because it's not a reflection on you. I just have a good rapport built up with Mike, and I think I'll be more effective covering this."

Steve Evans didn't have a good rapport built up with his *dog*, much less with a source. But I let it pass.

My phone rang. It was either Remington or someone else, I knew. Brilliant, right? Anyway, the question was, which would it be? I picked it up and answered, "Newsroom."

"Dunn, can you come by my office?" Singer asked. "I'd like to see you."

Singer never *asked* anything — and he especially never invited me to his office as if he were inviting me to dinner and a movie. I'd been hoping this call would come.

"Sure," I said. "I'll be there in five."

I hung up and grabbed my micro-cassette recorder. I rarely used it. I didn't tape council meetings or speeches. I usually consider recorders a crutch. I could write fast enough to keep up with most speakers, and that way I never had to worry about batteries or an equipment breakdown. But in special cases I'd bring the recorder along, and this was a special case.

I didn't know what Singer wanted, but I had my hopes. I told Sharon to let Barney know I'd made an appearance, and then I walked to my car. I drove to the station rehearsing what I would say to a guy I had once considered a close friend.

I didn't speak a word when I walked into his office. The look in his eyes made me forget everything I was going to say. I just sat down.

Singer reached into his briefcase and pulled out a folder. He put the folder on his almost-bare desk.

"I'm leaving my office for exactly ten minutes," he said. "I don't want to see you here when I get back."

He walked quickly from his own office. I stared at the desk and took out my tape recorder. Opening the manila folder, I hit the "record" button and started reading aloud the reports I found.

Wharton, Texas — a town about an hour away: Last September a gun store was burglarized. The alarm system was deactivated, and the locks were picked. The incident was followed by a string of residential burglaries; the residential burglaries were smash-and-grabs.

Bay City, Texas: In August a gun store was broken into, and more than three hundred weapons were taken. Again the alarm was neutralized, and the safes were opened as if by experts. Another string of sloppy residential burglaries followed.

Four other series of burglaries, all in different areas of Houston. All the same sequence. Gun store, then homes.

The next report was a log of names along with police records. Frank Johnson was about the third one down. I read off the names and the records. Daniel Taylor, nineteen: convicted of theft of a motor vehicle on June 1 of last year; probated sentence. Andrew Adams, twenty-three: possession of an unlawful weapon, aggravated assault — the victim was his common-law wife, it seems — and a neat list of other convictions. He'd spent almost two years as a guest of the Texas Department of Corrections in Huntsville. Frank Johnson, nineteen, no warrants, no convictions. Benjamin Stock, twenty-two: aggravated assault of a police officer four years ago. He'd stayed clean since then. Robert Hale, eighteen: already a couple of weapons charges. John Hobson, twenty: theft of a motor vehicle, multiple counts of burglary of businesses. A busy guy. Hobson too had spent a few months as a client of the TDC. The lists didn't have their juvenile records, but my guess was these weren't exactly choirboys.

The next item in the folder was a single photograph. It showed a black sedan — it looked like Sandersen's car, but I wasn't sure — stopped at some urban intersection. The street signs were clearly readable. A blond man — again, maybe Sandersen — was either giving or taking a dark briefcase from a black man dressed in a jogging suit. I described every detail I could find into the recorder, including the license plate of the sedan and the kind of coat the blond man was wearing.

There was one more thing. It was a letter from Captain Ed Clark, expressing the support and endorsement of the Police Officers Association for candidate Mike Sandersen. Clark asked officers to let him know if they were interested in donating time or money to Sandersen's campaign.

I read the letter into my recorder as fast as I could. My ten minutes were almost up. I switched it off, put the folder back on the desk, and left as quickly as I could. Singer wasn't in the squad room when I went by, but Clark's door was closed. Singer was probably in there to keep the captain busy for a few precious minutes.

I drove to my apartment, vaulted up the stairs, and sat down at my kitchen table.

For more than an hour I transcribed the tape into a spiral notebook. Every detail, every spelling, every word. When I was done I slipped the notebook into a stack of sailing magazines piled at the end of my couch. I put the tape and the recorder back into my coat pocket.

I grabbed the phone and dialed Remington's office. She answered.

"Singer has redeemed himself," I said. "Come by my house as soon as you get off work. I'll be back here by 5 P.M."

"I'll be there," she said.

I drove back to the office. The rest of the day I sat at my desk tapping a pencil against my computer keyboard. I didn't get much work done, but then my mind was on anything but work. I was starting to see a pattern emerge; I was starting to understand a little more about Mike Sandersen. But the fabric was tight, like the good canvas that makes a reliable sail. Everything was double-seamed and strong, secure. Sandersen's operation was very, very clean. Everything I had and everything that Singer had given me added up to very little. I needed more help.

I reached for my phone and dialed David's beeper number. When the tone sounded, I dialed my own number, then hit the pound sign. It beeped again, and I hung up. A few moments later David called.

"What's up?"

"David, can you come by tonight? I need your expertise."

"Sure. What time?"

"Make it about 7," I said. I might as well spend a little time catching up on things with Remington.

We hung up, and I looked back at Steve.

"How's that article coming?" I asked.

"Fine," he said. "I'll have it in on deadline. How about yours?"

"I'm stuck on a word," I said. "Problem is, it's the first word. So I'm a little behind."

Sharon laughed, but Steve ignored me and kept typing away.

Barney never made it in that day. He called from East Texas, where he and his wife had gone to see her parents, to say that he'd be a little late in getting back. He asked if I'd mind putting some of the inside pages together in the morning — Friday, when we do the Sunday paper. I told him it wouldn't be a problem. I wasn't surprised. But since I was officially the "assistant editor" — again, great title instead of great pay — I really couldn't complain.

Before long it was 4:30, and I decided to call it a day. If I hadn't written a single word by now, I certainly wasn't going to write anything between 4:30 and 5. Sharon waved as I left. Steve continued to ignore my existence.

As I drove home it started to drizzle. I turned on the wipers and continued on.

Remington was waiting in her car, under my carport, when I arrived.

"I got off a little early," she said. "My editor left at noon, so I took off too. She'll never know."

Again I wasn't surprised. The day after Christmas isn't usually a particularly productive one. We walked up the stairs and went inside.

"Can I fix you something?"

"How about some coffee?" she asked. "I'll help."

It was getting downright domestic in that little kitchen when I finally thought to tell her about Singer. With coffee in hand, we went into my living room (four paces away) and I played the tape for her.

"Departmental pressure," I said. "From higher up. Nothing he could do, but the way he's building that file I think he's planning to go to the D.A. with it. And with weapons involved, he could bring in the Feds. He said something funny to me about not feeling bad about burying those reports after he drank, smoked, and shot some targets. He doesn't smoke. I think he was trying to tell me he may attempt to bring in the Bureau of Alcohol, Tobacco and Firearms since weapons are involved."

"There are just too many loose ends," she said. "We've got to have this tied up in a nice little package, with every question answered. And we've got to have proof."

I nodded.

I looked at my watch. David wouldn't be here for about two hours. I had a task to accomplish *now*, I thought. Something had been bothering me since last night's drive home from Dallas . . . Something I knew I had to do.

"Remington, tell me about him," I said.

She looked up at me.

"Don't do this to me," she said. "We're getting along so well. Don't bring this up."

"OK, then I'll start," I said. "Her name was Julie. We met in college, in an art course. I was taking it for an easy A, and she was taking it because it was her major. She was very pretty, very eclectic, and a little dangerous. We went out once and decided that we didn't bore each other. That was probably the real basis of the relationship. It was enough, we figured. We made quite a pair in the conservative little Baptist college I went to. We got engaged not long after that.

"About six months later I was done with school, and I got the job down here, through the Texas Press Association. She'd never heard of this town. She had another couple of semesters to go, so we just called each other a lot, wrote a lot, and I drove up when I could. I should have known, but I didn't see it coming. She wasn't the kind of girl that sits home alone on weekends. She asked me if I wanted the ring back. I told her to keep it. I didn't want to see it again."

Remington didn't say anything for a few moments.

"Did you love her?"

"I guess so," I said. "I don't know. I didn't feel much when it happened. I wasn't furious or heartbroken or anything. I just felt a little depressed and a little tired."

"I know the feeling."

"Then what was his name?"

"Mark. He was a banker. I guess he still is. My father introduced him to me, so I should have known better. But I didn't. He took me to all his parties and dinners with bank executives; he seemed to like the fact that I could carry on conversations with his bosses. I didn't want to be a trophy, Emerson. Even when he asked me to marry him, it felt like he was doing it as a career move. I said yes because no one had ever asked me before and I was starting to get a little worried. That's stupid, I know, but he was handsome and intelligent."

"What happened?"

"I would notice him looking at other women, and I couldn't help feeling he was comparing me to them, to see if he'd done the right thing. And then one night when we were at a party, I watched him across the room talking to another woman, and I had this vision of me, twenty-five years later, divorced and stuck with a house that wasn't nice enough for him anymore."

"Like your mother."

"Like my mother," she said. "I didn't want to hurt like that."

The next part was going to be difficult. I could see Martin's eyes as he had watched my face in the study.

"So this wasn't really about you and Mark, was it?"

"What?"

"You broke it off because of your father."

Remington's eyes snapped up to meet mine. "I'm not particularly interested in being analyzed right now," she said. "I love my father, and this had nothing to do with him. He couldn't help it if Mark was a jerk."

I nodded and sipped my coffee, giving Remington a chance to go on. People usually do.

"So what are you saying — are you saying my father is ruining my life?"

"No, I'm not saying anything like that. Let me just ask you this: have you ever really forgiven your father?"

"Has he ever really deserved it?"

"That's beside the point," I said. "Have you ever really done it? I mean, just told yourself and the world that you feel what he did was wrong but you forgive him anyway?"

"Have you?"

Never ever, *ever* trust journalists. Just when you think you have them, they turn something around into a question and you're toast. I should have learned by now.

"No," I said after a pause, "I haven't. I think Martin was right. He told me I'm still blaming God for my engagement breaking up."

"So what can you do about it?"

"I guess I can forgive God," I said. "Just like Martin said. One of his more annoying traits is that he's very often right."

"How do you do that? Forgive God, I mean."

"I guess you do it the same way you forgive anyone else. Make a decision, then stick with it."

Remington was silent.

"Maybe you're right," she said. "I still hate Dad sometimes for leaving Mom and being so successful without her. She's the victim in this, and he's living it up. It's kind of like what you were talking about in Sunday school that first week. The bad go unpunished and the good go unrescued."

"It's not always that way," I said.

"I know," she replied, smiling. "*I* got rescued."

She looked down again at her coffee cup. It was almost empty, as was mine. She stood, took my cup, and went into the kitchen to get us refills. It was kind of like Wanda's Truck Stop, where you get free refills, except that Remington had all her teeth and no tattoos that I knew of.

When she came back, she sat down again without looking at my eyes.

"Martin's usually right, is he?" she asked.

"Usually."

"So what do we do?"

"We forgive."

"Shall we do this as a toast?"

"Perfect," I said. "God, I forgive You for letting me fall in love with Julie and then taking her away."

I lifted my cup.

"Dad, I forgive you for dumping Mom," Remington said as she banged her cup into mine.

"I think that's theologically sound," I said.

David arrived a little after 7 P.M. He came up the stairs and knocked at the door. I let him in and got him some coffee. We were starting our second pot.

"Come on into the kitchen," I said as we stood in the middle of it. "You two sit down, and I'll map it out for you."

For the next fifteen minutes I told them a tale of greed, racism, treachery and murder. There it was, laid out on the table like a big jigsaw puzzle. The only problem was, there were quite a few pieces missing. We decided to take them one by one.

First, the gas station.

"Easy," Remington said. "Gas stations are an easy way to launder money. So much money flows in and so much gas flows out, you can run a great deal of dirty money through even a small gas station. Didn't you ever wonder why Sandersen, a businessman, would let a bunch of skinheads run the place? He wasn't worried about turning a profit. It was just a front."

"I can go along with that," I said. "They never seemed excited about making a sale, did they?"

It all fit, but it was speculation — every bit of it. The pattern was there, but the fabric simply refused to unravel.

"What about Timmy?" I asked. "Who pulled the trigger?"

"Let's look at Singer's list," Remington said.

I got the notebook from the stack of magazines and pulled the list from it. I gave it to Remington.

"These are the guys who held me," she said. "This guy, Andrew Adams, is the leader. He's the one you called Adolph."

"Yeah, I thought he might be," I said. "Nice list of accomplishments. He beat up a girl and carried his shotgun to work with him. What a guy."

"Frank was on duty the night Timmy was killed," Remington said. "But when they were holding me, he seemed the most scared. I don't see him as the killer type. He's a joiner, I think. He probably just joined in the skinhead group because they'd have him."

I nodded. Most of these guys probably were just joiners. A kid without much of a future can usually find someone to blame it on, and the skinhead groups gave them entire races to blame it on. It was hard not to feel sorry for a lot of these kids. Frankie probably had a mother and father who loved him. Adolph might even have had a dog that put up with him. I kind of doubted that one though.

"What about Adolph?" I asked. "I mean, Adams."

"Maybe," she said. "But he did a lot of ordering people around. He might have been along for the ride, but I doubt he pulled the trigger."

"Who was the first guy I hit?" David asked.

Remington looked up. "The one who went into the gas station when they thought you were a customer? I think that was someone they called Benny."

"That would be Benjamin Stock," I said. "Age twenty-two, already busted once for assaulting a police officer. Shooting a retarded kid wouldn't be out of his league. Let's put a check mark by his name."

"He had the .38," David pointed out.

"That's right," I said. "There was no ballistics report in Singer's file though. Chances are the gun never made it to the lab. This case got sat on before Singer could send it out. That's one for their side."

That left one item — the photograph from Singer's folder. David's photos from the raid proved that the car was indeed Sandersen's car, and the guy was almost without question Sandersen. The street signs showed that the handoff took place near downtown Houston. We didn't know who the black man was or who was giving or getting what.

"I give up," Remington said. "What's a nice Nazi like Sandersen doing talking to a black guy?"

"I don't know," I said, "but there's got to be some reason the photo was in Singer's file. For one thing it means Singer or one of his detectives was trailing Sandersen; they must have suspected him already."

"So where does this leave us?" Remington asked. "What now?"

David looked at me too. They hoped I had an answer. I didn't.

"As far as I know, nothing has changed," I said. "We still have no hard evidence. There's just no solid proof. So we wait. They'll make a mistake. They're bound to."

I turned to David.

"I have a hunch about the photo," I said. "I need your help. When are you going over to Ruth's again?"

"Probably tomorrow night," he said. "Why?"

I told him what I needed. In college they make photojournalism majors take about as many journalism classes as they make us journalism majors take photography classes. In other words, one. But I knew David could do the job; it just required a little legwork. And being as he was my own personal — and somewhat lethal — Dr. Watson, I knew he'd do it willingly. I also knew he'd be much more effective than a skinny white boy like me.

"I want three confirmations," I said. "On tape. We can't go to the D.A. with anything less than that. Get photos of the ones you talk too. We might need art later."

I sounded much more confident than I felt. Actually I felt a little nervous; I might have even doubted there would *be* a later. But David nodded and even looked a little pleased about the opportunity. Still, there was one more thing I figured I'd better warn David about.

"Sandersen and the cops are ready to forget about the other night," I said. "But that doesn't mean the skinheads are. These aren't the kind of guys who let a few broken bones go unavenged. We'd better watch our backs. And until something breaks we lay low. Remington, that includes you. Don't deal with Sandersen any more than you have to."

"I'm covering his campaign," she said. "I'll have to see him some."

"No more than you have to, OK?" I begged. "Let's let him think he's won — at least with you. He knows he's got to take *me* out sooner or later."

An hour later David left, saying he had an early-morning photo assignment the next day. It had to be Mr. Andrews or Steve who set it up; I liked David too much — and knew him too well — to make him work before 10 A.M.

Remington looked at me with a hint of a question in her eyes. I knew what was coming. And I knew I'd better not blow it this time.

"Well, I guess I should be going too," she said.

"You don't have to. I was just thinking . . . let's go see the boys and get some schnitzel."

She smiled. I didn't blow it. This sensitivity thing wasn't so tough after all. However, I still refused to wear pastels.

Fifteen minutes later we were seated at a booth surrounded by tables with chairs turned upside-down on them. We'd caught the boys just as they were about to mop. Bad timing, *very* bad timing. Walter got this smug look when he let us in; the price tonight, he was saying, would be the dining room — swept and then mopped.

"That's fine," Remington said as she walked past him like a

cold northern breeze. "I'll show you boys how it's done. You could use a lesson or two."

Gunther rolled his eyes. Walter was set off again.

Dinner now? No, no, no, his body language insisted.

"If I need a lesson, well then, I had better learn it now and not spend any more of my wretched life being ignorant," he said. "Dinner can wait. Knowledge must come first!"

Remington nudged me when I started to say something — what I was going to say, I had no idea — and then she took over.

I sat in a booth with Gunther. Our feet were up on our benches, and we just tried to keep quiet and out of the way as Walter followed Remington across the dining room as she swept and mopped the place in record time — and with good results apparently. Walter found precious little to fuss about. He was looking over the poor girl's shoulder every step, taking in every stroke of the broom or the mop.

When she was done, Walter conceded defeat.

"It is adequate," he said. "I would have spent more time, of course, but I am a — what do you call — perfectionist."

"You tell us this? This we know," Gunther said.

"You would have *wasted* more time, you mean," Remington said. "Admit it. I did as good a job as you — and in less time."

Walter grumbled and said something about getting dinner; all this talk made him hungry. Gunther followed, starting in on his older brother in German — no doubt making the most of Walter's moral defeat.

"Where did you learn that?" I asked as Remington sat beside me.

"High school," she said. "I was a waitress after school for two years. At night when we closed and cleaned up, I always had to do the floors. I got pretty good at it. Quick too. Not a particularly glamorous skill, but always marketable."

I laughed. This girl was funny. She had the one quality I looked for most in a person — she didn't take herself too seriously. At work every day I was confronted by people who did.

Politicians, some cops, school board members, teachers, even the city's animal control officer. When the city council overreacted to a report that a twelve-foot python had bitten a child in Dallas, council members decided to pass an ordinance banning pythons and boa constrictors that were longer than ten feet. They discussed and debated this ordinance for weeks before finally voting. After a unanimous vote, the animal control officer, who was sitting in the audience, raised his hand.

"Have you got a question?" the mayor asked.

"Yes sir," this guy says. "I just want to know whose job it is to measure the snakes. Is it me or the code enforcement department?"

Remington, Andy, and I didn't stop laughing for a full five minutes. Neither did the rest of the audience. Good old Mayor Sam was banging the gavel and probably would have jailed us all if he was a judge. The animal control officer just looked confused.

Remington's story the next day was as funny as the incident itself. Not only could the girl mop, but she could write. Before the burglaries started and Timmy was killed, I had always thought Remington was entertaining. I was starting to think even more highly of her now.

The schnitzel emerged in about ten minutes. Walter was still eyeing the floor, looking for streaks or spots or any place Remington had missed. We'd had more than our share of coffee already that night, so we only stayed long enough for dinner. As we left Walter made it a point to open the door for Remington, something even I hadn't done yet.

"Our restaurant is your restaurant," he said. "Come and mop any time."

She curtseyed and walked out the door. I grinned at him as I left.

"That means they've accepted you," I told Remington as we got into my car. "You're now one of their special customers."

She didn't come up when we got back to my place. It was already past 11 P.M., so she said she was going on home. I nodded and turned, very effectively avoiding that awkward moment at the end of a date when you're expected to put your lips on each other. I try to avoid such moments. When I put my lips on someone I want it to be because I feel it's time, not because it seems the thing to do at the time. If that makes sense.

As she drove off she waved. I waved back and started up the stairs. As I started to unlock my door, I noticed something different about it.

A black swastika was spray-painted on it.

Call the police," Martin said.

I had called him as soon as I got inside. He seemed the logical person to talk to. The numbness I felt went deep into my soul.

"And call David," he added after a moment. "I don't know if the police will be any help, but you'd better warn David that he might get some visitors. Emerson, do you want to stay with us tonight?"

"No, I'll be fine here," I said. "I think this was just a warning. If they wanted me, they could have just kicked open the door and waited inside. Thanks for the offer."

I did as Martin said and called the cops. They said a patrol car would be by in about five minutes. I made a quick call to David and waited.

A knock at the door told me that either the nice guys in blue or the Nazis in black were here — maybe both. Apparently I couldn't trust either group. It was a cop, however, and one I felt I could trust: Nix. She was apparently still on the evening shift.

She took a report — when did I leave, who was with me, when did I come back, did I know where my downstairs neighbor was, all of that — and then asked me if I wanted to request close patrols for the rest of the night. That's where a cop car drives by every fifteen minutes instead of once a week (that was about the average in my neighborhood).

"No, I think the kids have had their fun for the night," I said.

"Then take a ride with me," she said.

I looked at her closely. She looked a little scared but determined. Her eyes told me that whatever was going to happen was for my own good. I said OK.

I followed Nix down the stairs and into her patrol car. I sat in front. As she got in she said into the radio microphone that she was going ten something or other for thirty minutes. I think it was cop code for eating dinner. She turned off her car radio and the radio she wore on her belt.

We drove through the side streets and residential streets for about fifteen minutes before she began talking.

"It's not Singer," she said.

"I know."

"Higher up . . . much higher up. Do you have a gun?"

I started to get the feeling that the conversation wasn't going to be pleasant.

"No."

"I won't tell you to go out and buy one, but I will tell you to be careful. Do you know what's going to happen to this vandalism report?"

"I can guess."

"You're right. And you can expect the same kind of help if — or when — you have more trouble."

"Obviously not all the officers are going along with this."

"Most aren't," she said. "At least most don't want to. But orders are orders, and if we're told that the purse-snatching at the grocery store takes a higher priority, that's what we work on."

"What have the officers been told about me?"

"That you're going to be working for Walter Moore, the funeral director who's going to be running against Sandersen. And that Moore wants to cut the salaries of police department personnel, and maybe even downsize the department itself.

That you can't be trusted; that you'll be doing your best to discredit the department."

"Do you believe that?"

"No."

"Is Remington a target?"

"Not now. So far, she's 'played ball,' according to Sandersen. I don't know what that means, but I can guess."

"So how does it feel to let a gang of skinheads run wild in your city?" I asked.

"I'm here with you now, aren't I?"

We'd come almost full-circle back to my apartment.

"Is Singer going to the county or to the Feds with this?"

"Depends on how much information he can get," she said. "And it depends on how long he can hold out. He's not taking this well. He's not the kind who sits by and lets this sort of thing just happen."

She stopped the car at the curb in front of my place.

"Emerson, be careful. You're a good kid. I don't want to see you hurt."

"You watch yourself too," I said. "You took quite a risk taking me for this little ride."

Then it occurred to me to ask why she hadn't just said all that in my apartment. The night suddenly got even colder.

"Does this mean my apartment isn't . . . secure?" I asked.

She didn't respond.

"And my phone lines?"

"Just be careful, Dunn . . . Very careful."

Then she drove off.

As I walked up the stairs, I caught a glimpse of my sailboat, sitting on its trailer behind the carport. I had a tarp over it to protect it from the winter. The sails and ropes were all inside, neatly folded and coiled and stored. I wondered if Remington liked sailing. I wondered if we'd ever get the chance to find out.

The next day was Friday — time to put out the Sunday paper. David had the typical "day after Christmas" shots of Christmas trees being dropped off at the city landfill, and Steve had his story on Sandersen. Again he sounded like a peach of a guy. I was getting a little sick of it. But I knew better than to complain aloud, in front of anybody anyway.

I had a couple of stories from the police blotter. Thieves had stolen a family's new TV and VCR but left the new bicycle and BB gun. And a jewelry store had been broken into on Christmas Eve. Some people have heart, others don't.

A story on a house that burned to the ground because of faulty Christmas tree lights rounded out the cheery edition. David had some good shots of the family sifting through the debris looking for anything they could save.

By late afternoon Barney still hadn't shown up. That was becoming more and more typical; he was trusting me more with the paper. He wasn't concerned that I might not get the paper out; he was more worried I'd let something slip through that Mr. Andrews wouldn't approve of. And on several occasions I plotted to do just that. But in the end I usually realized that the job market for journalists was tight, and I very much enjoyed eating, even if it was just microwave burritos. So Barney knew I wouldn't take too many risks with the paper or with my job.

Barney called at about 6:30 P.M. to say he wouldn't be back that night. He asked if there were any problems. I told him not to worry. I had most of the pages built and the headlines written already. I knew I could be out of there by 8 P.M. if Barney wasn't around to get in my way. He said he'd OK some overtime for me and hung up.

Steve was finishing the story on the house fire, so I had a few minutes to kill. I reached into my desk to get my file on Sandersen — the one I kept at the office.

It was gone.

"Steve, have you seen my Sandersen file?"

"Nope," he said, not looking up. "I've got my own."

Sharon was wrapping up the classifieds for the evening, so I looked over at her.

"Sharon, has anybody been through my desk lately besides me?"

"Not while I've been here," she said.

I let it go, but made another entry on a mental list that was growing quite long and revealing.

By 8:30 — OK, so I was off a little — I was done and the pages were ready for Jimmy. He loaded up the van and left while I locked the place up. I was home a few minutes later. Before I'd been there thirty seconds, however, the phone rang. I answered.

"Emerson, I received an interesting call," Remington said. She sounded a little scared.

"Hold it, Aggie," I said. "This line isn't necessarily secure."

She paused.

"Neither am I," she said. "My hair never does right, and I think my chin is too strong for a girl. Where can we meet?"

"Sunday school," I said, trying to think of a place close to her. "We'll get the lesson ready for Sunday."

"Have you got a key?"

"Yeah, from days gone by when I was a regular. See you in fifteen minutes."

I was already in the parking lot when Remington drove up.

She was wearing a dress — a navy blue one, with gold trim on the lapels, very nautical looking — and her trench coat. She looked as if she were going out on a date.

"I think your chin is fine," I said as she got out.

"Thanks. What's this about your phone line?"

"Inside," I said.

I let us into the church and started to walk around to the right of the foyer, toward the Sunday school rooms, when Remington grabbed my hand.

"In here," she said and led me into the sanctuary.

"Why here?"

"It's so pretty," she said. "Don't you love it?"

I hadn't thought about it, I guess. I looked around at the maroon carpet, wooden pews, and matching pulpit. The drapes were fading and no longer matched the carpet. The hymnals stuffed into little racks at the back of each pew were tattered and badly in need of replacement. The organ was new, however, and the decorations dressed the place up a little.

"It's just like a little country church," Remington said.

"It *is* a little country church. What's the big deal?"

"You don't see it anymore, do you?" she asked. "You get used to it, I guess. But everything seems so much different in here, different from out there. Out there, everything is rotten. You have to be a cynic to survive. In here it's not like that. In here people care about each other. And something more is offered. Wouldn't it be nice . . ."

"Wouldn't it be nice if what?"

"I don't know," she said. "I think I was going to say wouldn't it be nice if it were all true. But now . . ."

"But now you're sure it's *not* true?"

"Something like that," she said. "You believe, don't you? You've seen everything I have, but you still believe."

"Is it that hard?"

"I guess not," she said. "I guess I just hadn't given it much thought."

"That's how it was for me," I said. "But once I started thinking, there were just some things I couldn't get around."

The conversation went on for more than an hour. We sat on a pew halfway down on the right side, looking up at a wooden cross above the empty pulpit. She held my hand most of that time. It was as if Remington wanted to wrap herself in a blanket of God before we talked about why we'd met here.

Mostly we talked about the basics: forgiveness, what Christ did, and what it means to us now.

"Does He feel real to you?" she asked. "Does it really feel like He's nearby? Like all the songs say?"

"Yeah," I said after a moment. "Much more so lately than in the past few months. But I think it was more that I was avoiding Him than anything else."

"And you've stopped avoiding Him?"

"Finally . . . I think sometime during Timmy's funeral I realized that I'd let myself drift away. But that's the great thing about God. He'll take you back."

"But I've avoided Him all my life."

"No problem. At least not for Him. I think it makes it a little tougher for us though. I came to Christianity late; we adults are a little more stubborn about admitting our needs and shortcomings. There's a little bit of pride we have to give up; once we surrender that, it gets easier."

She thought about that for a moment.

"It just seems a little too easy," she said.

"What a cynic. Think about it some. There really aren't any hidden clauses. I promise."

It got quiet again.

"Tell me about the call," I said after a few minutes of silence. The silence had meant two things. First, that our talking about the subject of God was over, for the moment anyway. She'd learned about all she could absorb right now about my faith. And second, it meant we weren't doing anything with our lips, and that situation was starting to become uncomfortable as several options presented themselves. My question snapped her back to the present.

"Sandersen says that since I'm now on his side, I might want to watch you. He says you might be dangerous."

Those were my exact thoughts about five seconds ago, I wanted to say. But I didn't. I was busy being sensitive.

"So what do you think you should do?" I asked instead.

"I was hoping you'd know," she said.

"We could stop seeing each other," I said. "That would make Sandersen and our respective editors happy. At least for now, while we're waiting for this case to break."

"That's an option," she said. "Telling Sandersen to buzz off is an option too."

"No. I'm already a target, and so is David. You've got to keep clear of me for a while."

She was silent.

For what had been such a promising evening, this was turning out to really stink. But I had to continue. I told her about the swastika and my conversation with Nix.

"Don't call me until I give you the all-clear," I said. "I've got a bad feeling about this. We're up against some powerful people."

"So that's it?"

"I guess so."

"What about Sunday school? Won't you still need me?"

I sighed. She had me there. But I couldn't risk it.

"No, I'll do fine," I said. "But I sure will miss you."

That seemed to kill the conversation. Remington said it was getting late and that she'd better go. I nodded. We locked up the church, and I walked her to her car.

She looked at me but didn't say anything as she left.

It was a long drive home for me. I walked up the stairs to my apartment and found a note taped to my door. It was from my landlord. He said he highly disapproved of my door decoration and that he wanted the door repainted by the end of the weekend.

On Saturday cold winds and rain combined to add insult to injury. I didn't leave my apartment once. I stared out the window, I slept, and I thought. Mostly I thought about Timmy. Remington had never known Timmy. I never knew him well. I let him check my oil, I said hello on those rare occasions when I went to church, and that was about it.

What had he done that made someone want to kill him? The skinheads — if they indeed pulled the trigger — couldn't have had much reason to hate him. He was white, he did what they said, and he was dumber than they were. That must have made them feel a little bit better about themselves.

Maybe they were afraid he'd overheard something. Or maybe he saw something. Who knows?

I tried to read some, to watch an old movie on my black-and-white TV set. Neither activity worked. I missed Timmy, I missed Remington, and I missed my dog.

Airborne got his name one afternoon when I took the eight-week-old golden retriever to the boat yard with me. I was still in Dallas with my parents then, and I belonged to a small sailing club in Arlington. I had to do a little work on my sailboat, and I brought the puppy with me to keep me company. The boat yard was empty as I drove up. What would be the harm in letting the puppy run around for a little while, I thought to myself. So I took off his leash and let him roam.

Within seconds he was on the dock, eyeing the ducks in the water eight feet below. No one had told him he was a duck-retrieving dog by heritage, but I guess he had figured it out on his own. I heard a series of very bold barks, and I watched this puppy leap from the dock toward the closest duck, which was already paddling away. It was a swan dive of Olympic quality. He hit the water and came up barking and paddling furiously.

I'm not quite sure what he would have actually done with a duck had he caught one, but he seemed to have big plans. Luckily the ducks were quite a bit faster than he was, this being his first time in the water. I retrieved him and kept him on the leash after that. But the name Airborne Ranger stuck.

He was no longer a puppy now. He was four years old (he's a lot older in dog-years, but then so am I). *I need to get that dog down here,* I thought, watching the rain.

The telephone was as silent as I was all day. If anyone had any more answers than I did, they sure weren't calling to share them with me. David was probably with Ruth today. I had no idea where Remington was or what she was doing.

At about 9 P.M. I decided to stop feeling sorry for myself and go to bed. It didn't work; I lay in bed thinking the same kinds of thoughts. I was no closer to proving that Timmy's death was more than a robbery gone bad. I *was* closer to finding myself in a similar position. I knew the swastika on the door was a warning. I also knew that I was a significant liability to Sandersen's political goals. Sandersen's skinheads — the shock troops of the white-collar white supremacists — would be happy to eliminate that liability for him, I was sure.

I looked around my darkened bedroom. In a corner, next to a glove and a potato sack full of baseballs, stood a bat. That was as close as I had to a home security system. And I wasn't any good with it, even on the field.

Eventually I dropped off to sleep. I heard the alarm go off, and

I was almost glad; at least I had something to do that day — even if it was taking on a class of junior high kids by myself.

I got to the church about five minutes before class started. The room was almost full. Most of the conversation I overheard as I walked in dealt with Christmas loot. Kids. When they saw me walk in, they hushed, as if maybe they were starting to enjoy the class. Yeah right. They were probably just afraid some girl named Aggie was going to deck them. They watched the door as I entered, looking for her. Dennis raised his hand.

"Where's Ms. Remington?"

I didn't have a good answer for him. I said something about her not being able to make it today. He nodded.

"You guys break up?" he asked.

Remember what I said about the Gypsies?

"No, we didn't break up," I said. "We were never together to begin with."

He nodded again, then turned to the boy next to him, a kid named Randy.

"She trashed him," Dennis said in a stage whisper. "Ripped his heart out and stomped on it."

The class lost all semblance of discipline. I fondly remembered David's commando tactics and wondered why he wasn't using any of them now on these kids. Dennis was explaining, in a loud voice no less, the agonies I must be going through, but how I must be used to this sort of thing by now, while Samantha was arguing that if anyone had done the dumping, it had been me, since I was such a great catch. After Dennis and Randy disagreed vehemently, she slugged them both. I thanked her for defending my honor and ego and raised my voice.

"Let's get on with it," I said.

The next few minutes seemed like dog-minutes. We talked about New Year's resolutions. For a while the kids were almost serious. Dennis talked about how he needed to get his grades back up; he resolved to study more. Another one of the kids resolved to not argue with his parents so much.

"What about you?" Samantha asked me.

This kid would make a good journalist, I thought to myself. *She's just sneaky and mean enough.*

"I don't know," I said. "I guess I need to make my appearances at church a little more regular. You guys have any ideas for me?"

"Yeah," one of the kids said from the back row. "Get Ms. Remington back here."

"I'll work on it."

"How about your wardrobe?" one of the girls asked. "You could resolve to buy some shirts that aren't either blue or white oxfords. How about some pastels?"

They must start 'em young, teaching them how to make men's lives better through the Power of Pastels.

"No way," I said.

That was pretty much the end of the Bible study. The last ten or fifteen minutes of class was taken up by a discussion about what faults I could work on for the next year. If I took all their advice it would be a very busy twelve months. Still, it was all good-natured, and I *had* made the mistake of asking.

After church I went to Martin's again. It seemed the only warm place in the city. I knew Remington was better off staying away from me, but that didn't mean I had to like it.

I took Ricky to Martin's house in my car. We talked for a while about the usual stuff. He told me what he got for Christmas, and I had to explain to him that when you get old, you don't *mind* getting shirts instead of trucks for Christmas. When we got to the house he helped me set the table. Before long the girls walked in, followed by Meg.

"Before you ask, she didn't dump me," I said to Meg. "The kids in Sunday school already grilled me."

Meg smiled.

"I didn't think she would," she said.

"Now wait, that wasn't meant to imply that there was ever any relationship to dump," I said quickly.

"Hmmmm," she said.

"Anyway, we just felt it would be best for her to lay low for a while. Sandersen's been telling her to stay away from me, that I might be dangerous. I don't want her in the same kind of position I'm in."

"When did you decide this?"

"We decided together, last night," I said. "She got a call from Sandersen, then we met at the church and talked it out."

"Emerson, this is a very delicate time for her," Meg said slowly. "She's dealing with a lot of new things — risk, Christianity . . . and you."

I didn't say a word. I seriously doubted the last entry in Meg's list. I didn't see a girl like Remington getting too worked up over a guy like me. But Meg was right about the other two. This was probably the first time Remington had ever been in any danger. She was OK for now, but when Sandersen found that he hadn't really bought her off, he'd be a little upset. Mixed in with all of this was that first, inexplicable attraction to faith. Most of us latecomers remember the feeling; it's an uncertainty, a knowledge that we somehow can't stay on our own little islands of reality. We can see the outlines of a beckoning coast through the mists.

For me, that feeling lasted about a month. It had happened when I started a new job in a small town outside Dallas. My publisher asked me if I'd like to visit his church. I was still a confirmed disbeliever, but what do you tell your boss? I agreed, and a couple of Sundays later I snuck into the evening service and found a back-row pew to myself. There were about fifty people there for Martin's sermon. I don't remember much of of what he said, but I remember the feeling I left with — a feeling of confusion. Having become a cynic at a young age, I'd always assumed there was a basic constitutional separation of church and brain. Martin proved to be a very well-educated man, not anything like what I guess I had expected a preacher to be. Suddenly I saw my own accepted version of reality for the island that it was. I kept coming back for more sermons, more off-key singing, and more clearing of the mist between me and the coastline. Within a month I was ready to make a decision.

Remington didn't seem ready for a decision yet. Martin hadn't pushed her, and neither had I. Maybe that was a mistake. But Meg was right. Remington was at a delicate stage. All I could do was trust God to take care of her.

Martin walked in, and we talked about church matters for a while. The kids were playing in the living room; the newness hadn't worn off the Christmas toys yet.

After lunch I washed the dishes and made excuses to leave early.

I wasted the rest of the day back at my apartment mostly the same way I'd wasted the day before — feeling sorry for myself. I was getting pretty good at it. I fired up the coffeemaker just so I could stay awake a little longer and steep myself even deeper in self-pity.

Monday came with little fanfare. I was dreading Tuesday; Tuesday night was New Year's Eve, and I didn't have a date. The fact that I didn't have a date didn't bother me as much as the fact that I didn't have a date with a certain person; and later on it bothered me that that bothered me. On Monday we stayed busy getting as much of Tuesday's work done as we could, to make Tuesday a lighter day. Barney and his wife were going to a party Tuesday night, and if Steve had condescended to speak to me on Monday he probably would have told me he planned to watch TV with his parents on New Year's Eve. But he didn't.

By 6 P.M. Monday we had everything pasted down except the front page; we could do that before noon on Tuesday. We all left together — Barney, Steve, and me. Our sports writer (really a part-timer who was finishing his degree at the University of Houston) had, as usual, gotten done early and gone home already. Will, a tall, lanky guy with a full beard and a South Texas twang, wasn't much of a socializer. David had also finished early. He'd told me to give him a call if I wanted to do something after work. I think he could tell I was a little down. I told him I'd phone if I was up to it, but I doubted I would be.

As we locked the door behind us and Steve walked to his car, Barney asked if I was all right.

"I'm fine," I said. "It's just the weather. It's been drizzling for a week now."

"Yeah," he said. "It gets to me too."

He started to say something else, but stopped.

"What is it, Barney?" I asked. Barney paused and watched Steve drive off.

"It's Mr. Andrews," he said after a moment. "He's asked if I've got a file built."

I knew what that meant. "Building a file" is what some companies do when they're having problems with an employee. They carefully document each transgression and mistake; that comes in handy if the employee sues for improper termination when he or she is sacked. I knew Andrews had been burned once before — by an editor who had been sacked, then took the paper to court and won. Andrews would be very careful about firing anyone else.

"What did you tell him?" I asked.

"I told him I didn't, and that if I did have a file I wouldn't have anything to put in it," he said. "You're the most dependable reporter I've ever had. But, Emerson, he's getting weird about this. He asked me to watch you very closely. It might not hurt for you to start sending out some resumés. This might prove to be terminal."

I nodded.

"I'll watch myself," I said. "January isn't an easy time to be looking for a job. Maybe he'll come around."

"Maybe."

Barney didn't look as if he believed that. I thanked him for the information, and we left.

Tuesday was an easy day. We had the Thursday paper built by 11 A.M. instead of noon as we'd predicted. Mr. Andrews didn't come out of his office once, not even to survey our work before it left for the printer.

I spent Tuesday night — New Year's Eve, mind you — alone. David stopped by and told me he was going into Houston, to go to a party with Ruth.

"It's at the Jewish Community Center," he said. "Come on, man — free food. Kosher too. I know you like kosher food."

I laughed. "You go on. I'll be fine here. I've been craving a BLT, and I doubt I'd find one there."

Still, it was nice of him to stop and check on me. I just felt like being alone.

I spent most of the evening thinking about the case. I went over the details again and again. One thing that didn't add up was Remington's relative safety. Why was Timmy killed but Remington spared? They didn't even *touch* her when they held her at the station for three hours. It didn't make sense. Maybe it *was* just a robbery gone bad. But I couldn't shake the feeling that there was a link.

I thought about spending some quality time with Dick Clark, but I fell asleep before the ball came down in Times Square. As I drifted off, I wondered if Airborne was watching the ball drop (he seemed to like television more than a dog should). I wondered if he realized that seven balls were dropping for him. I wondered if he missed me.

New Year's Day was a holiday at work (except for the circulation department, which had to get the Thursday paper distributed before Thursday morning). I called David to make sure he'd made it home OK from Houston. He had. He asked if I'd like to come over for some lunch, and the offer was tempting, seeing as how his mother was cooking fish. I declined in order to keep my brand-new tradition of spending holidays feeling sorry for myself. I napped most of the day. It was that same tired feeling I had when I'd broken up with Julie. I couldn't explain it, but since no one was around I didn't have to.

The rest of the week was like a black-and-white movie you've seen a dozen times. It was flat and colorless; any feelings it should have conveyed had long since faded with repetition. It was a dull march through the days, then straight home at night to sleep the sleep of the just — or at least the sleep of the justifiably depressed.

On Friday night I was partially awakened from this zombie-like state when Barney did something strange — he did all the work.

"You go on home, Emerson," he said at about 6 P.M. "We can take it tonight. Get some sleep. You've been looking tired lately."

"Sleeping is about all I've done," I answered. I was getting a little worried, but figured I'd better go along with it. It just wasn't like Barney. I started to realize that something was up. "You sure you have things under control?"

"Yeah," he said. "Scoot."

I left, wondering what the problem was. Maybe he was going to train Steve to do some editing and layout, and he didn't want me to be around to see it. Or maybe he was just being generous.

I went to bed by 9 P.M. and slept until noon on Saturday. Even when I awoke, I felt tired. I spent the rest of the day watching old black-and-white movies, ones I'd seen a dozen times.

Sunday was brighter; at least the sun was out. It was almost heartening as I looked out my window when I got up.

I'd gotten a lesson together on forgiveness — not that I was a big authority on it, but I must admit that I gave God plenty to forgive. ". . . that grace may abound . . ."

Anyway, I stuck to a few verses from the New Testament. Mainly I planned to talk to the kids about what it means to forgive — that it's an ongoing thing. I was learning that myself. A few times during the past week, deep in my depression, I had felt myself slipping back into the old resentment. I fended it off by reminding myself that I'd already forgiven everyone involved.

After an interestingly Jewish breakfast — a bagel, some cream cheese, and even some lox that David had brought me — I grabbed my Bible and headed for church.

The drive was cold and a little lonely. Remington hadn't been helping me for very long, but I sure had come to depend on her.

I ducked into the classroom at about 9:10 A.M., before most of the kids had gotten there. I sat back and waited as the room started to fill. Dennis came in about five minutes after I arrived, so I talked with him about school and his New Year's resolution. He said his main problem was that he was flunking English. I told him to call me later in the week and we could get together — grammar isn't nearly as complicated as they try to make it seem in school, and I had a few tips I could pass along. Grammar ain't that hard.

When the 9:30 bell rang, I stood and walked up to the lectern. I hated lecterns. I didn't like anything between me and whoever I was talking to. So I told Dennis to get rid of it.

"Like out the window?" he grinned.

"No," I said. "Like over in the corner . . . There."

I pointed. But when I turned back around to face the class, I looked into a pair of eyes as blue as the waters off Galveston Island.

"Hello, Remington."

She came into the room and took her usual seat in the back.

"I thought we had all this worked out," I said.

"Free country," she said. "Freedom of religion . . . It's there in the Constitution. So stop wasting time and teach."

An hour later we were alone in the classroom.

"Why are you here?"

"Because I want to be," she said. "Sandersen may think he's bought and paid for me, but I'm not going to give this up for him. I think I like it here."

"Do you have lunch plans?"

"Not a thing on my calendar," she said.

"Good. Martin says Susie's been asking about you."

Remington was a big girl, I told myself. She knew what she was doing. Sandersen wasn't going to like what she was doing — specifically, hanging around with me — but deep down I knew she wasn't the type to buckle under to him.

She was glad we were going back over to Martin's for lunch. I think she saw something in his family that she'd lacked in her own. She definitely saw something in Meg. Reporters as a rule ask a lot of questions, but she was really quizzing Meg. She helped Meg warm up lunch, and the two left Martin and I out of the conversation completely. That was OK. Martin and I went out to his study for a few minutes before we sat down to eat.

"Have you gotten anywhere on the case?" Martin asked when we sat down.

"No, and neither has anyone else," I said. I told him about my drive with Nix. He looked a little worried.

"Does that mean your apartment might be bugged?"

"That kind of thing is rare," I said. "It takes a boxful of court orders to get it approved. But it's possible. It's also possible they wouldn't wait for approval — or even bother to try to get it."

"Would Sandersen want you that badly?"

"I don't know. Maybe."

Ricky appeared at the door to tell us lunch was ready. We followed him in and found chicken and dumplings waiting. Meg's dumplings were legendary — no one dumpled like she did. She also had a cake prepared for dessert; this was living!

But as hard as I tried, I couldn't ignore the fact that Remington was sitting across the table from me and was upstaging the meal. You know you're in trouble when a dame starts attracting more of your attention than a home-cooked meal does. I tried to concentrate on the dumplings, but it just wasn't working.

To my right sat Ricky; Susie was next to Remington. At least Ricky had some loyalty. He and I discussed dumplings. We both decided that "dumpling" was a dumb name; nothing gets dumped. Meg, for example, might *lower* the dough into the broth, but it was a very graceful — might we say artistic? — maneuver. It was nothing akin to dumping. I told Ricky about David's mother's matzo-ball soup, which I explained to him is sort of a Jewish version of chicken and dumplings. We decided that "matzo ball" was at least more descriptive than "dumpling" — and certainly more polite.

I figured he was a preacher's kid; he could deal with the theological implications later.

Theology is exactly what Remington, Meg, and Martin were discussing. Remington was asking some very good — that means hard to answer — questions about Christianity. She certainly didn't plan to walk into anything blindly. Martin was having a ball. I remember talking about the same things with him about five years before.

Martin had answers then, and he had the same answers now. I listened quietly. The answers still rang true. I might have been away for a while, but I hadn't really left anything, I realized gladly.

Before long the afternoon was turning into evening. We had coffee as Remington continued questioning Martin. When we were done, she and I washed the dishes and talked for a few minutes.

It was a little uncomfortable being that close to her. She didn't seem to notice.

"These are good people," she said.

"I know."

"They're happy."

"Not always," I said. "It's not always easy."

"Marriage or their faith?"

"Both, I guess."

We finished up in silence. Remington was working hard to assimilate everything Martin had said. It was a lot to take in, I realized. Apparently she realized that too.

"My roomie in college went to church," she said. "She'd try to get me to go. I'd always have some term paper to work on though. Once she brought me a tract. I read it and decided I wasn't looking for comic-book Christianity."

I smiled. "Tracts have their uses," I said. "But I know what you mean. I can remember sitting in Martin's office one day and finding a tract called *The Four Spiritual Laws*. I read through it and decided I'd done all that. Then I found a tract called the *Seven Steps to Salvation*. I wondered which three I'd missed."

She laughed. Martin, who was passing through on the way to his study, gave me a look that said something to the effect of "you might want to take that stuff a little more seriously." I grinned innocently at him.

We finished the dishes and wrapped up the evening. We thanked Meg and Martin, hugged the kids, and left.

I avoided the temptation of asking Remington over. I didn't think it would be a good idea. Maybe I still needed some time alone.

I got it. It was vastly overrated.

Monday dawned clear and cold. It wasn't a productive day. I went into the office long enough to punch out a story on how local retailers fared during the heavy holiday buying; a mall that opened up closer to Houston was drawing quite a bit of business away, and retailers weren't happy. It was an interesting story, and luckily it took most of my day. That way I didn't have to think much — about the case or about Remington. I finished the article at about 4 P.M.

Steve, who'd said not a word to me that entire day, was still working hard. Barney had shown up for a few minutes but saw that I had things under control. He sat around for a while trying to look as if he was being useful. He wasn't fooling anyone. But like I said, he's a nice guy. So when I finished my article I talked with him for a while. He told me about his in-laws' spread in East Texas — pine trees, red clay, and not much else, but it was still East Texas and a beautiful place to be.

When everyone else started filing out the door, we left too. Steve stayed to work late — I don't know why. I really didn't understand him lately. I went on home and even thought about buying some paint so I could cover up the swastika on my door. (I'd missed my landlord's deadline, but missing deadlines was a matter of pride with me. That was about the only thing I did well and regularly.)

I figured I'd better stop by the house to see what color the door was — I couldn't remember if it was white or off-white or something else (maybe even some obscure pastel shade of white). You know how complicated these things can be. But when I arrived I saw that lovely couch inviting me to drop in for a rest. I accepted.

A knock came at my door a little after 8 P.M. It was probably David and Ruth, stopping by on their way back to Houston, I thought.

I was wrong. It was Benny. Benny looked a bit bashed. His left arm was in a cast. David had done that, I realized. I hoped Benny was left-handed.

"Come take a little ride with us," he said with a surprising amount of politeness and good grammar. "Mr. Sandersen wants to talk to you."

I looked out onto the small landing outside my door. Two other punks stood behind Benny. I got a bad feeling. Remember, Benny was the guy who had pulled a gun on me once and who probably wasn't happy about the cast on his arm.

The other two guys were familiar. I didn't know their names though.

"Sure, boys," I said, "I'd be glad to. I'd like to talk to him too. Let me get my coat."

Benny's eyes narrowed, but he was obviously under orders to behave himself — for now, at least — so he just nodded.

I got my trench coat — it seemed Bogartly appropriate somehow — and I considered stuffing my bat into a pocket. They'd probably notice, I thought as I passed it by. I was on my own. I turned out my kitchen light and locked my door as I followed the three skinheads down the stairs. They walked toward a black sedan. *That means they really have come from Sandersen*, I thought to myself as they opened a door.

"Nope," I said, "we'll take two cars. That way if the date doesn't work out, I can leave by myself without hurting your feelings."

That didn't seem to be part of their plan.

"Get in the car," Benny said threateningly. Apparently Sandersen's orders were simply to get me there, and suddenly Benny seemed willing to do it on either a dead or alive basis if I didn't cooperate.

"OK," I said. "But don't think this means you get to kiss me good night when you drop me off."

My head hit the roof of the sedan as Benny helped me into the backseat. I don't think he *wanted* to kiss me. Well, he was sure ruining his chances if he did.

A punk got in next to me, while Benny and the third skinhead got into the front seat. Benny drove; the other two remained silent. They were two of the guys who hadn't given us any trouble when we'd liberated Remington — the only two still healthy, I realized. I think the guy next to me was the one David stepped on after the cops arrived; I wasn't sure. Like I said, they all looked alike.

He did have an interesting wardrobe, however. The Nazi SS insignia — the skull and crossbones, a real original idea — was mounted in silver in a pin on his jacket. He also had a silver cross pinned beside it. What a combination. I didn't mind so much that David had stepped on him.

Benny drove down my street and onto Commerce Street. But instead of heading north to the gas station, he went south — as if to my church. Maybe the cross was winning out, I thought. But when we reached Border Street and turned east, I started getting nervous. The church was to the west; Remington was to the east.

"Boys, where are we headed?"

No one said a word.

"You guys don't like me much, do you?"

"Shut the Jew-lover up," Benny said. The guy next to me nudged me. *I could take him*, I thought, and I think he probably feared the same thing. So he just nudged me and hoped I'd get the message. I didn't.

"Is that it? Is that all you can find to hate about me? That I'm a Jew-lover? Come on, I'm a white boy just like you. I've got short hair, I'm not a Communist, and I don't have a black girlfriend — at least not currently. I'm just like you."

The second guy in the front seat turned around.

"No, you're not," he said. "We're Christians."

That shut me up. I had forgotten how painfully that word can be twisted. White supremacists, I remembered, often think of themselves as good Christian Americans, fighting the tide of racial impurity threatening to tear apart the country. I'd even heard some use obscure Bible verses in an attempt to justify their beliefs.

The car smelled like leather, and the boys seemed to have matching black-leather jackets, the kind bikers find stylish. I tried to ignore the fact that we were nearing Remington's apartment complex. But I felt real fear for the first time that night when we drove in and came to a stop just below her door.

"Sandersen's a little old for her, isn't he?" I asked.

The punk beside me nudged me again, harder than before. This time it hurt.

David once told me there's no such thing as a little war. He told me about the Jews who held out in the Warsaw ghettos, waiting for the inevitable as Nazi tanks moved through the streets trying to "sanitize" the region of Jews. He told me of the bunkers, the secret meetings, the sacrifices made by a few who simply refused to submit. They knew they had a choice: march onto the cattle-cars and die in some concentration camp, or die in their own streets gunned down by Nazi storm troopers.

The Warsaw holdouts didn't add up to much, so the Germans

brought only a small contingent of soldiers to do the job. They brought a few men, but the Jews gave them a war. It was the Nazis' first defeat — if only a moral defeat. Within a few weeks the ghettos were razed.

With my side aching from the kidney shot I'd received from the skinhead, I decided that maybe these boys needed a war. It was just a matter of waiting until the time was right. And I knew it would be my kind of war, not theirs.

"Come on," Benny said as I was led up the stairs. A single knock later, Adolph — I mean Andrew — opened the door. I was pushed into the room.

Remington looked mad. She wasn't hurt, but she wasn't having a nice time either. She sat on one end of her couch and Sandersen sat at the other, smoking a very large cigar. It was a dark-leafed Churchill — named in honor of the late British Prime Minister who liked his cigars big. I smiled.

"Good evening, Mike," I said. "What can I do for you?"

Sandersen leaned back and looked at the end of his cigar. He wore a suit — as always — but his tie was loosened and his usually immaculate hair wasn't. He looked like he'd had a long day and was ready to get business wrapped up quickly.

"I want you to realize who you're dealing with," he said. "Just in case you haven't gotten the message yet."

I was standing just inside the door, with Benny and the two other punks surrounding me. I felt a little claustrophobic, so I nudged them aside — nudging my seatmate a little harder than the others — and walked over to Sandersen. On closer inspection I noticed a bulge in his coat, just under the hankie in his breast pocket.

"Do you mind?" I said as I reached down and lifted his lapel. With my left hand I deftly lifted what I knew I'd find in the inside pocket — another cigar. I dropped his lapel and stood looking into his amused eyes.

I didn't turn around, but I could feel the large, bald bodies behind me, ready to turn me into Spam. Sandersen waved them away.

"A light?" he said.

"Please," I replied, biting off the end of the large cigar. I didn't make it a regular habit of indulging, but cigars are a very viable means of communication. A cigar says, "I'm successful, I'm confident." How do they say that? you ask. Very simply I might answer, smoking a cigar says, "I can afford to offend everyone within smelling distance. I simply don't care."

I took a puff and sat down in a recliner across the coffee table from Sandersen and Remington. Remington was looking at me as if I were crazy.

"Now," I said, "tell me who I'm dealing with."

Sandersen laughed. "I could learn to like you, Dunn," he said. "As much as I could like anyone who befriends Jews and tries to corrupt honest young women like A. C. here."

"Yeah, I can just see us as bowling partners or fishing buddies," I said. "So what do you want from me? Need some help for your boys here? I think veterinarians have stuff now that cures mange or whatever it is that's wrong with their hair."

I took a puff and let it out slowly. Sandersen was getting tired of calling off his dogs.

"Get out of town," he said. "There's a new order here, and you don't fit. You're a good reporter — you can find a job anywhere . . . Anywhere but here."

"I don't know, I kind of like this place," I said. "Hot and muggy during the summer, cold and muggy during the winter."

Sandersen paused. He was getting tired of me. "What's your price?"

"Your soul," I said. I think I meant it.

He waved at his boys. I felt a hand grab my right arm, and I was helped out of my seat.

"This is going to be a warning," he said as I was escorted away.

There were several disappointments that evening. The first

was that Sandersen didn't let me keep the cigar. The second was that I lived.

I woke up in Martin's living room. Remington, Meg, and Martin were in the kitchen; a demolition team was in my skull. Benny had done most of it himself. It was all fairly tame as far as maimings go, since it was all done in the short drive from Remington's place to my curb, where they considerately dropped me off. Or out, to be more exact. Adolph had driven while four of us occupied the backseat: Benny, another punk, me, and Pain. Benny, as it turned out, was right-handed; the cast on his left arm didn't seem to slow him down any.

My final thought as they rolled me out of the backseat onto the cold ground in front of my apartment was that I was very glad I had bled on Sandersen's shiny new car. Then I went to sleep.

32

"You look terrible," Martin said as he came into the living room.

"I'll be fine," I said, sitting up. "How's Remington?"

"A little scared," he said. "A lot concerned."

She came into the room with Meg. It looked as if she had been crying. It was nice to know I was appreciated.

I heard Remington's side of the story. She insisted that she never felt as if she were in any danger; Sandersen just seemed to drop by for a visit. He mentioned that he'd heard she'd gone to church with me again, and he was concerned that I was still "after" her. She said she doubted it, and he said something to the effect of "let's invite him over and find out." Then he sent his boys over. And after his boys left, Sandersen stayed and chatted with Remington while I was being pummeled — just as if he and Remington were old friends and nothing bad was happening. When the skinheads came back, Sandersen politely left. He even emptied his ashtray. It was clearly a warning to her.

"Emerson, Sandersen told me to give you a message," she said. "You're supposed to pick up an envelope just like mine at the gas station tomorrow — on your way out of town."

"Am I going somewhere?"

"I think you should," she said. "I think you're just going to be asking for more of this if you don't."

"Naw, they need me at the paper," I said. "And the kids in Sunday school need me. And my landlord needs me. If I weren't there, he might actually find someone who pays the rent on time. Then what would he gripe about in his spare time?"

Still, I looked at Martin. I didn't have to ask, and Martin didn't have to be asked. He knew his role, and he knew his words were going to be final. If he said stay, I'd stay; if he said go, I was out of there.

"Emerson, how's your faith holding out?"

I grinned through a broken lip. "I've got enough to see me through," I said.

I slept on Martin's couch that night. Remington was back over first thing in the morning. She took me to my apartment and dropped me off. I spent about three hours cleaning up — more specifically, soaking in a hot bathtub. Remington had been right in not calling the cops or an ambulance — since they're on the same radio frequency. But this was going to take an awful lot of aspirin. After I soaked for a while, I took a quick strategic nap on the sofa. My body seemed to need it more than I did, but I went along with it.

It was after 4 P.M. when I finally dressed and drove to the office. Paula might be a little mad, but since I had a council meeting that night she knew I'd be working late.

I walked in the front door and went straight to my desk. Steve was in, Barney wasn't. Nothing new. Steve was ignoring me, as was Paula. That was fine; they usually did anyway.

Sharon was looking at my face — the boys had left a few marks, mainly a split lip. But Sharon didn't say anything to me about that; she just kept looking. After a moment she told me I had three messages. Something in her voice sounded strained.

"Yeah?"

"The first is from Bill Singer," she said. "He said he had a 3 P.M. meeting, but he wants to talk to you after that. He also said something else. He told me to tell you that the ballistics report came back. It was a .38 special slug, but not *that* .38."

Then Benny's gun hadn't shot Timmy, I thought. Maybe Benny wasn't such a bad guy after all — excepting for the fact that he had made my face and abdomen into oatmeal.

"The second message?"

"David called this morning, says he has three," she said, looking down at her notes. "He wasn't making much sense. He said two are homeless, one is a grocery store clerk."

I smiled; Sharon didn't. Now I knew something was wrong. If Sharon didn't have a little fun with David's enigmatic message, she was really bothered.

"The third message is from Mr. Andrews. He wants to see you as soon as you get in," she said sadly.

Sharon immediately looked away. I knew what was coming, and so did she.

I figured I'd better call Singer first. Any talk with Andrews was liable to take a long time. I dialed the direct number to Singer's office, but the dispatcher answered.

"Police," she said.

"Singer please."

"I'm sorry, but Bill Singer no longer works here," she said. "Can I direct your call to another investigator?"

I paused. Bad sign. Very bad sign.

"No . . . thanks," I said and hung up.

I walked back to Mr. Andrews's office. The door was closed, so I knocked. I heard a muffled "Come," so I went. He sat at his oversized desk, which was covered with area newspapers, the incredible amount of mail a newspaper gets every day, and a check made out to me. One of the first skills a reporter develops is reading upside down — it comes in handy when talking to some official at a desk. I've read entire full-page memos while carrying on a meaningful conversation with the mayor.

We'd just been paid last Thursday, so I knew the check wasn't a good sign. It could be a bonus, I thought. But I doubted it.

"Mike Sandersen says he won't file charges on you for last night," Andrews said.

This was indeed going to be interesting.

"Last night?"I asked.

"He told me about how you went to his gas station drunk and picked a fight with his clerks. It looks like you lost."

"Well, you know, drinking is a regular habit of mine. That and picking fights with gangs of racists."

Andrews glared at me.

"I think he's being more than fair. Under the circumstances I'm going to have to let you go. You've been a good employee and a hard worker. You can stay here this afternoon and use our computers to work up a new resumé, and I can write a letter for you. But you're just not effective in this position anymore."

Sandersen wanted me out, and he knew three strikes just might do it: the threat of further pain, the loss of my job, and the very tempting offer of cash in a little white envelope I could pick up on my way out of town.

I didn't respond immediately, so Andrews handed me the check. It was more than a month's pay. Andrews was being generous. His tone softened.

"You're just too ambitious," he said. "This is a small town, not some big city like Houston. We don't have the same kind of problems they do, and we'd like to keep it that way."

I didn't understand what Andrews was rambling on about. I usually didn't. But I accepted the check, nodded, and stood to leave.

"I hate to do it, Emerson," he said.

"I know. I know."

I walked from his office to my desk. Sharon wouldn't look me in the eye. I surveyed my belongings: a small rack of reference books, a plaque for second place in some contest, and a trophy for first place in some other contest. The trophy wasn't bad, I thought. The article that won was a city budget story — they have contests for the most readable and least boring budget stories. Good idea, I thought. Anyway, it was a brass trophy of a lady wearing a sheet and wings. I don't think she was an angel. I think she was called "Winged Victory" or something inane like that. I called her Martha. She was the first trophy I'd ever won. I wasn't much of an athlete in high school and in fact wasn't much good at anything else either.

I went back to the darkroom to get a box. David picked up his developing chemicals in Houston in bulk and usually had a few large boxes around. I found one marked "Toxic/Extremely Hazardous" and went back to my desk. Cleaning out my desk took about fifteen minutes. When I was finished, people were starting to leave. Donna, the ad rep, left, and Paula left; both said nothing to me. Maybe they'd heard and believed the part about the drunken brawl. A few moments later Andrews walked out of his office, dropped a typewritten letter on my desk, took his coat from the rack, and left. He didn't say a word. The letter was functional. It said I had worked for him for almost two years and that

I was a hard-working, dedicated employee and that he was sorry I felt it necessary to resign and move on. Interesting angle, I thought. I didn't remember a thing about resigning.

I turned to my computer and called up my secret file. Barney actually had access to everything in the system, but anything I wanted to keep private I put in a file called "Bond Election Issues." That's boring enough to keep anyone out of it. I had a fairly current and fairly complete version of my resumé typed in already. I knew it might be some time before I was around a good computer and laser printer again, so I revised it as thoroughly as I could and started printing out a few copies.

I felt a hand on my shoulder.

"I'm sorry," Sharon said. She held her purse under her arm. Her eyes were looking a little red.

"Let this be a lesson to you," I said. "Never come in to work after 4 P.M."

She smiled, and the threat of tears subsided a little.

"We knew you'd be late," she said. "Steve told us not to expect you in too early. But we didn't know to expect this until Mr. Andrews came out and made his big announcement just before lunch."

"Don't take it so hard," I said. "You'll probably miss talking to my mother more than you'll miss me."

Sharon laughed. It was easy to make Sharon laugh. That's what I loved about her.

I looked over at Steve, who seemed to be concentrating very hard on something on his computer screen.

"I guess this means a promotion, Stevie," I said. "I'll leave Mr. Potato Head in the drawer for you. The last assistant editor left him for me, so I think it's only fair."

"Thanks," Steve said without emotion and without looking at me.

Sharon hugged me and started to leave. She stopped at the door and turned to me.

"Will you be at church on Sunday? It was good to see you back there."

"Maybe once more," I said.

And now we return to that sorrowful demise I wrote of lo, these many chapters ago. It was after 6 P.M., and I was finishing a list of references and what had been a promising journalism career. I went over the list again; I listed some old bosses and Martin (it never hurts to have a pastor on your list of references — it makes people think you're a nice guy). I hit the "print" button and waited as the laser printer made a typeset-quality printout. A few seconds later I made about ten copies on the copy machine. Steve and I were alone in the office now. I put the handful of copies into my box and stared at my blank computer screen.

The market was tight. Journalism jobs aren't easy to come by, I realized. I could try the Dallas area again. My parents always had a spare bedroom for me. And for a few moments I even considered accepting that money Sandersen had waiting for me.

But no, that wasn't an option. I stood and started to leave. I looked over at Steve, who was still ignoring me. *He used to look up to me*, I thought. *He used to like me too.*

"See you, Stevie," I said.

"Yeah." He still didn't look up.

I shook my head and walked out the door.

Twilight and a chilling breeze met me outside in the parking lot. I set the box on the hood of my car as I fumbled for my keys. I must have been more affected by the day's events than I realized. My hands were unsteady. I dropped the keys. I bent down for them.

And for the first time in months I found myself on my knees. I suddenly didn't want to get up. I felt the weight of crushing, numbing defeat on my shoulders, and I realized that I had caused most of it myself. Singer was fired. Remington was the pawn of a man who wouldn't stop at giving her the same kind of warning he gave me the minute she stepped out of line.

Timmy Joyce was dead, and the one piece of evidence I thought I had — Benny's gun — wasn't the gun that killed him. I had nothing.

I don't remember praying. I just remember sagging against my car, wondering why I couldn't get up, and then wondering why I wanted to. My head still throbbed from the beating I'd gotten. My soul still ached for everything I hadn't told Remington yet.

And then I knew.

Just like that I knew. The confusion lifted like an early-morning fog from a peaceful harbor. I stood and took my trophy from the box. I walked the five paces over to Steve's car.

"You're a good boy, Stevie," I said. "You wouldn't keep anything nasty around the house where Mom could find it, would you?"

I bashed in his driver's side window with the brass trophy. Martha wasn't even scratched. I tossed her aside, brushed away some of the glass, and unlocked the door. The seat was covered with glass, but it wasn't the seat I was interested in. I reached down and felt around underneath it. I found what I thought I would.

"You're also not the type to keep this sort of thing in your trunk, are you, Stevie?" I said to his car. "It's too new a toy for you. You'd want it near you, easily accessible."

I quickly located a Smith and Wesson .357 Magnum. It didn't bother me that the gun wasn't a .38. I knew a .357 can use .38 Special bullets; the chambers are close enough in size. I stuffed the pistol in my belt, drew my jacket over it, and walked back into the newsroom.

"Just forgot to make a call," I said as I walked to my desk. I dialed David's beeper number and then waited. He must have been near a phone — he was probably at the dinner table, I realized — because no more than thirty seconds later he called.

"I'm at the office," I said. "I need you."

Steve looked up.

I reached down and dialed another number.

"Hold your editor there for fifteen minutes," I told Remington as she answered at her office. "Offer her money, chocolate, anything. I'll call."

I hung up and looked over at my former coworker.

Steve's eyes narrowed. As he reached for the phone, I reached for the gun.

"You messed up, Steve," I said. "You knew too much. When did he sway you? And what was it specifically that won you over? Did you like the idea of an Aryan Nation? Did he promise you that you could be his Minister of Propaganda when he heads the new Reich?"

Steve looked defiant. His blond hair was cut much shorter than it had been when he first came to work at the paper, and it was conservative even then. He'd gotten very suddenly cynical and unsociable. I wondered why I hadn't seen it before. He didn't say anything.

"I've had it," I said. "I've had a rotten day . . . And you're going to suffer for it."

I pulled back the hammer and cocked the .357. Steve started to look a little nervous.

"He must have gotten to you at that first press conference," I said. "Or maybe even before. Maybe you live down the street from him. I don't know, and I don't care. But you were so ready to join his club that when he asked you to ice Timmy as your initiation, you complied, isn't that right?"

"Prove it," Steve said.

"You did it yourself, the day I reported it. You said it was a shame they killed him for less than $150. The police report didn't give a specific amount. The attendant — that was your friend Frankie — didn't even know himself how much was taken.

That's probably because he can't count that high. The only one who knew how much was taken was you. So you had to be involved. That's the way Sandersen works. He makes you as dirty as he is himself. That's why Remington has been safe all along — he thinks he's soiled her with his money. And you killed for him."

Steve was silently glaring at me. He wanted to run, he wanted to jump me, he wanted to make a quick phone call. I wanted him to talk.

I raised the weapon and aimed at his face.

"I have nothing left to lose," I said. "And I've got a message for you from Anna Joyce, Timmy's mother."

Tears started welling up in Steve's eyes; it was either fear or regret. Steve hadn't yet seemed to be the kind that regrets much, so my money was on fear. But I sincerely hoped it was regret. I walked a few paces toward his desk. He was frozen in position. He closed his eyes as the cold steel of the barrel touched the bridge of his nose.

I paused a minute for effect.

"Anna says she forgives you."

I lowered the gun.

Steve stayed frozen for about fifteen seconds more. Then he opened his eyes and looked up at mine. His weren't the eyes of a bad kid; at least no more bad than any of us. But maybe that's just a cynical journalist's opinion. He'd been easy prey for Sandersen . . . naive, dissatisfied, looking to belong to something. He'd probably never held a gun until Sandersen put one in his hand.

"Will you talk? I can promise you protection — from your friends, not from the law," I said.

Steve said nothing for a moment.

"You can't protect me from them," he answered very slowly and very quietly.

David entered the office.

"But he can," I said. "And there are others."

David looked confused. I motioned for him to sit down.

"Talk," I said as I pulled my tape recorder from my jacket pocket.

It was a story of steady dehumanization. The rhetoric is clear: They just aren't as intelligent as Us. They aren't even really human. Jews, blacks, Hispanics, everyone else. Even one of their own race — Timmy — wasn't really a person. He was little more than a smart dog, they told Steve. Timmy was a dumb animal. And he was a dangerous animal. They wanted Steve to prove himself, so they let him eliminate the problem of Timmy. Steve said that at the time, he felt detached, like he was watching a movie. When the gun went off, it was like a random explosion in his hand. He saw Timmy fall, but it didn't feel like he'd done anything to cause it, Steve said. It was only later that his actions started to sink in.

Now he had plenty to say.

Fifteen minutes later I dialed Remington again.

"Let me talk to Jane," I said.

"She's a little annoyed," Remington said. "She wants to know what this is all about. So do I."

"Then pick up the other line," I said.

Jane Dodson answered with a curt "What can I do for you?"

I didn't know Jane well, though I respected her about as much as I respected Remington. They put out a competitive newspaper with half the staff and half the number of editions. In her editorials she usually sided with the Chamber of Commerce and the town's well-entrenched Establishment, but at times — every once in a while — she would buck it a little. From what Remington told me, she was more a newshound than a manager, so her people skills left a little to be desired at times. But Jane was dedicated to the same things we were. I felt I could trust her.

I told her my story; it took about five minutes to outline it for her. I told her I'd been fired too. I figured she deserved the whole truth.

She paused when I was finished. "Confirmation?"

"Three witnesses from downtown Houston," I said.

"Who are they?"

"Two homeless men. We have photos of them to help us find

them later if needed. The third is an Asian who runs a grocery store in the area."

"The homeless aren't usually considered reliable witnesses," she said. "Do you have direct quotes?"

"On tape."

"I want confirmation on the triggerman's story too," she said. "If you can get that in the next hour, we'll go with it."

I could hear Remington's breath quicken. Remington loved a scoop.

"Save me the banner," I said. "And I want a double byline with Remington. I'd be proud to work with her."

"You've got it."

The next call I made was to the police station.

"Is Sally Nix on duty tonight?" I asked when the dispatcher answered.

"She's on northside patrol, sir," the dispatcher answered.

"We've got a vehicle burglary at the newspaper office," I said. "Could you send her by? She's good at working with distraught women."

It wasn't exactly a lie. There was a vehicle burglary — I'd done it myself with a brass trophy. And Nix *was* good at working with distraught women. I simply let the dispatcher infer for herself that a distraught woman was involved in said vehicle burglary.

Five minutes later Nix drove up. She must have been close by. David led her into the office.

"I have the whole story," I said. "We've got enough to go on now. This is Steve Evans; he's involved."

I paused. I didn't want to go on, but there was no getting around it.

"He's the one who killed Timmy," I told Nix. "Sandersen put the gun in his hand and told him to, but he pulled the trigger."

I looked at Nix as I handed her the .357.

"I need your help," I said. "We've got to get him out of here. He's going to be the first target when the trouble starts coming down."

The officer looked at me and smiled.

"You'd better come through for me," she said. "I can get him to Singer, and Singer can get him to the Feds. But you'd better not let me down. I'll be a target too."

So Singer *was* working this for the Bureau of Alcohol, Tobacco and Firearms. I felt a little bit better.

Steve stood as Nix cuffed him.

"You're doing the right thing, Stevie," I said.

He looked at me. "I know."

Nix turned to me before she led Steve to the patrol car.

"I had a feeling about you, Dunn," she said, nearing me.

I'd never been kissed by a heavily armed woman before. I was glad Remington wasn't around to see it. I hadn't thought about it before, but Nix wasn't bad-looking for a cop. She was a pretty, red-headed woman of about thirty-five, I guessed.

"Don't let me down," she said again as she started to leave.

I wasn't going to — you can be sure of that. As she and Steve left, I looked at David and grinned.

"Let's go get some gas," I said. "My tank's a little low."

Benny was on duty when we pulled into the gas station. Steve had told us he would be. Benny's first mistake was that he was watching television and didn't notice it was us until we walked in. Then he *noticed*.

I knocked the telephone off the wall with my baseball bat. The phone being a non-moving object, I nailed it pretty good. It sailed across the small gas station better than any baseball I'd ever hit — not that there were that many baseballs I'd ever hit, but that's not the point. I didn't want Benny making any telephone calls — at least not yet. David went to the back door and locked it, then came back up front to do the same to the front door.

Benny looked a little scared when he saw that this time he was alone and I wasn't. I went to the cash register and slammed it with the bat. It also being a non-moving object, unlike baseballs, I got another pretty good hit. A few more and the drawer popped out. Underneath the cash tray was a white envelope. I stuffed it into my jacket. Evidence, I swear — really.

"Don't worry, Benny," I said. "I've almost forgotten about last night. And I'm not here to hurt you. Not much anyway. I just want to have a talk with you."

Benny was silent as I pulled out my tape recorder. He seemed relieved when he saw it wasn't a gun.

"Listen to this," I said. I played Steve's confession. I could see Benny hardening as he listened. Benny, Adolph, and the rest of the boys were clearly identified and implicated on the tape.

"So what?" he said when it was done. I didn't rewind it. I knew I had more to add to the tape.

"So you've been a bad little Nazi," I said. "But you know, I think I'm going to let you go. And I'll even let you live. All you have to do is tell me it's all true and we walk out of here. If you don't, then you don't walk out of here."

"You can't do that," he said. "You can't get a confession under duress."

"I'm glad to see that your experiences with the law so far have taught you some nice legal terms," I said. "But we're not the law and we're not cops, remember? We're just a couple of reporters. A couple of wayward reporters yet."

I paused a moment, then said, "David, hold him." I'm a patient guy, but I didn't have all night.

David knew that my intentions weren't nearly as dastardly as I tried to make them sound; Benny didn't. Benny was the kind of guy who assumed that secretly everyone was as malevolent as he was.

"You'll let me go?"

"Yes," I said. "Just say the magic words."

I held the tape recorder and hit the red button.

"OK," he said. "It's all true. Everything Steve said. But we didn't kill no one . . . Steve did that."

I turned it off as Benny lowered his head.

"David, hold him," I said again.

Benny looked up and started to panic. David grabbed him in one of those pretzel moves they must teach you in the Israeli army. It didn't look comfortable. I fingered my baseball bat.

"Now I'm going to tell you the rest of the story, Benny. And I want to you take a message to Adolph for me."

Benny couldn't take his eyes off the bat. I put it down.

"Sandersen had you boys doing his dirty work," I said. "That part's on the tape. He'd buy a part-interest in a gun shop, open it up one night, and let you boys clean it out. He didn't want you to break in because, let's face it, you boys are sloppy. He didn't want to replace broken windows or a blown-apart safe or a crushed gun cabinet. So he'd let you in himself — and turn off the alarm himself — and you boys would make off with the guns. The next day the other owner or the manager would come in and report it as a very professional burglary.

"Now here's where he slipped up: being the part-owner, not only did he have keys, he also had access to the list of customers. There are federal forms filled out for every gun sale. He knew exactly where to find more guns because they'd been sold from his store. He knew the repeat customers had gun collections, so he knew just where to send you boys. What did you do — just wait around until the homeowners left for work, then bash your way in? That's where he made his mistake. That's what links him and you to the burglaries."

Benny wouldn't look at me, so I picked up the bat again. I held it gently to his stomach, right at the place that was hurting most on me.

"That's not the end of the story, Benny," I said. "Listen up — do you know where the guns are?"

"No."

"That's right, you don't. I can tell you where they aren't. They aren't being stockpiled for the day the revolution starts and the Aryan Nation becomes a reality. You thought the guns were going to the Cause, didn't you?"

His eyes narrowed.

"They weren't. As for Sandersen — I don't know if he's a member of the Aryan Sisterhood or the Overage Confederate Skinheads or the KKK or whatever it is you guys are, but he's not *really* one of you. Guys like Sandersen don't have causes. Guys like Sandersen have ways to make money . . . and ways of using people like you to help them.

"Here's what I want you to tell Adolph or Andrew or whatever his name is: Michael Sandersen was taking the guns you stole and selling them to gangs in Houston. He didn't even sell them to the white gangs; he sold them to the Asian gangs, the black gangs, the Hispanic gangs."

I pushed the bat into Benny's gut a little harder.

"Will you take that message to your friends for me, buddy?" I asked. "You see, it's going to be in the newspaper in the morning, but I'm afraid most of you boys don't read newspapers. I want them to know who they've been taking these risks for, what kind of person they've been helping out."

Benny nodded.

"And I need one more thing from you," I said. "Sandersen's telephone number. Not the number he gives out, the one that has the answering machine. I want the number you call when you have to talk to him."

A few moments later we were ready to go.

"We'll be seeing you, pal," I said as David let him go. David unlocked the front door, and we started to leave. Then I stopped.

"Oh, sorry about the telephone," I said. "There's a pay phone a couple of blocks up though."

David and I drove off. I dropped David at the office, where he was going to have the unique experience of printing up a batch of photos for the competing newspaper. He'd be over as soon as the shots from downtown Houston were done, I knew.

I drove to Remington's office. Nix's patrol car was there; she must have transferred Steve to Singer already. I knew Singer could take care of the rest. I walked into the competition's office (which had nicer chairs and desks than ours, plus newer carpet and actual drapes) and found Remington, Nix, and Jane the Editor waiting for me.

"I got it," I said. "David will be here with art in about half an hour."

For the next two hours Remington and I wove a tale of crime and dirty politics that would make a Chicago gangster blush. Mike Sandersen had cut a deal with the police department. The old chief was a hands-off manager and wouldn't have noticed any of this going on, so it did. Sandersen knew that Captain Edward Clark wanted to be more than just a lowly captain; Sandersen promised Clark that once he was elected to the city council, he'd see to it that the chief was fired. Clark, a longtime veteran of the local department, would be the perfect replacement. Clark went for it in a heartbeat. But he went too far. By ordering his officers to cover up a couple of burglaries, the kidnapping of Remington, and who knows what else, Clark had underestimated his officers. One bad apple can spoil the bunch, unless of course all the good apples have guns and connections with the Feds. The officers saw through the promises of raises and "better resources" to the kind of sickness that Sandersen was — the kind that can infect a whole town.

We wrote about how Sandersen drove his black sedan to his gas station, then put a gun in the hand of a lonely, scared young man and told him to kill a retarded guy. In Steve's own words, we wrote about how Sandersen talked of purifying the race and how someone like Timmy wasn't enjoying his life anyway.

We wrote about how Sandersen tried to bribe the press when his hoodlums got out of hand one afternoon and held a young reporter hostage. We wrote about how he used his influence and his firm, persuasive voice to convince a publisher of another newspaper to fire a reporter who "didn't want to play ball."

And we wrote about the arms deals and about how an Asian shopkeeper would see Sandersen make periodic deliveries to the neighborhood. The shopkeeper told about how the drive-by shootings started to increase when Sandersen started making his rounds. We quoted a homeless man who talked about waking one morning under a pile of newspapers only to see Sandersen unloading a trunk full of guns and bragging to another man about how he could get more.

We quoted another homeless witness as well. People like Sandersen never seem to see the homeless, though they're just a few yards away. But the homeless see people like Sandersen. David had done good work.

Nix was supposedly on patrol when she stopped in again. It still wasn't clear who in the department could be trusted and who couldn't. She just stopped in for a few moments, as if she was just making her rounds, but staying too long would look suspicious. Clark had made a lot of promises to a lot of people about promotions and power. But Nix wanted to see this through to the end. Before she left, she promised she'd be back at midnight when her shift ended.

When she came back a while later, she was wearing street clothes, but under her jacket she still wore her Glock 9mm automatic pistol.

Jane worked with us, catching our typos, correcting some grammar, and pointing out the holes in the story until it was perfect. David arrived with the photos. He had shots of my car gracing the garage out on Highway 6, shots of the Asian shopkeeper pointing to a bullet mark in the brick front of his store, and he even resurrected the shot of Sandersen and some unknown person examining the Uzi.

Jane was pleased. There was ink in her blood and fire in her soul. I could see why Remington wasn't in a big hurry to work for a larger newspaper. Jane Dodson knew her business; she made sure we used enough direct quotes and that we used the word "allegedly" enough to cover ourselves.

She put a headline on the story, pasted it down, and put the page into a box with the rest of the Thursday edition.

"I'm off to the printer," she said. Their newspaper was printed near Clear Lake, which was about half an hour away. "You two have done a great job. If we get sued or go to jail over this, I just want you to know something." She grinned at us. "You'll both be fired immediately."

Nix stopped her before she left.

"I'd like to see this thing all the way through," Nix said. "I want to go with you to the printer, if you don't object. I'm not going to be able to sleep until I see this in print and on the stands."

Jane nodded. Nix turned to me. I sincerely hoped she wasn't going to kiss me again, especially since Remington was standing there.

"Take care of her," Nix said, nodding over at Remington. "She's had a rough couple of weeks."

"Yeah," I said. "I'll do what I can."

The two older women left. I wasn't sorry to see that Jane had an armed escort, and I had to admit I wasn't planning on getting much sleep either until I saw the paper in printed form and on the stands.

Remington came over and sat beside me.

"Is it over?"

"Not yet," I said. "I have one more call to make."

I reached into my jacket and got the phone number Benny had so kindly given me. I would guess it was a portable phone that Sandersen kept with him at all times. He sounded as if he was in bed when he answered.

"Mike, this is Emerson," I said. "I have some sound advice for you: get up, get dressed, and find Singer and the ATF before your boys find you. They know about the gun sales to the minorities, and you know how they feel about minorities. They're not going to be happy with you."

Sandersen paused, then hung up.

I didn't much care whether he followed my advice or not. The whole lot of them would probably be in federal custody by morning. With Steve's cooperation the Feds could have warrants within a matter of hours.

Remington was still sitting beside me — uncomfortably close. I wondered what Martin would do in a situation such as this. But then I decided to ditch that and do what I should have done a couple of weeks ago.

It seemed warm and sunny for a January day as Remington and I drove around town — in her car, which had a heater (that might have something to do with the warmth, but not necessarily). We drove around looking at newspaper stands. In each one that held the *Courier*, we read the bold headlines. Everyone else was reading the headlines too. There are things a newspaper can accomplish overnight that would take a matter of months or years for our slow-moving legal process. By noon the entire town knew about Sandersen's dealings. Clark held a press conference denying involvement but resigned by 5 P.M.

Sandersen was in federal custody by that evening as well. His boys were being rounded up on burglary and aggravated assault charges by the locals.

I called Sharon at the office. Andrews had been called up to the corporate headquarters in Houston to answer to the CEO generally about the case and specifically about why I was fired and why the other newspaper broke the biggest story the town had ever seen.

Sharon made it clear I should stick around town for a few days. She sensed a resignation coming, and the new publisher would probably love to have me back. Sharon always knew the Status of Things, so I trusted her.

Singer was back in his old office by Friday. When I went to see him, there wasn't much to say to each other. We'd each done our part, and Bill wasn't the kind of guy to get mushy, so before long he was back to speculating on the professions of several of my ancestors.

It was good to have him back.

Four months later, on a bright, beautiful spring day, I finally popped the question to Remington. It had been a nice four months, I might add. I'd seen Remington really start to grow in her newfound faith. It was taking the edge off her cynicism, and I think maybe mine was starting to dull a little too.

But back to that important question.

"Remington," I asked, "do you like to sail? Because I have this boat, and the water's just about warm enough."

Remington just smiled.